SAVANN

MIDNIGHT
MAGIC

S. Lee

Midnight Magic

Clover Pack

Book Two

Savannah Lee

Savannah Lee

Midnight Magic: Clover Pack Book 2

Copyright © 2023 by Savannah Lee

All rights reserved.

Inquiries: savannahleenovels@gmail.com

Cover Design by JV Arts

Editing by Wildfire Editing

Formatting by Unalive Promotions

Interior Art by Saralyn Everhart with Crafted Chaos

To my readers,
Thank you for all the love.
This one is for you.

Midnight Magic

CHAPTER ONE

Holy. Fucking. Shit.

What did I just get myself into?

Darkness enveloped me as I stepped through the portal, a frigid sensation coursing through me for only a moment before light blossomed again. The feeling vanished as quickly as it came, and I found myself in an entirely new world from the one I had just left. My eyes darted back to where I had just come, locking on Oliver's through the now-wavering portal. Panic etched across his face as a deafening blast echoed from his side, the edges of the portal rapidly diminishing as his concentration waned.

"Go, I'll find you!" His voice reverberated through the glimmering haze, sounding more like a ghoulish echo than a man as the portal snapped completely shut, disappearing as if it had never been there in the first place.

I stood slack-jawed, taking in my new surroundings. I craned my neck to gaze at the sky, two colossal moons hanging equidistant from each other. Their azure glow painted everything with an otherworldly hue. The rugged and barren landscape stretched before me, marked by jutting rocks and patches of stone. A gentle mist kissed my skin, and I gasped as I discovered an ocean just a few feet behind me, the rocky area I stood on serving as the shoreline. It was unlike any ocean I'd ever seen, its water a royal plum, eerily still, making no sound. Its surface was like glass, smooth and unmarked. I would have attempted to walk on it if not for the slight waver at the water's edge where it lapped at the craggy beach.

As I stared out at the water, a sense of calm fell over me, when I should have been feeling anything but. The water, the moons—everything about this place should have unnerved me, but it didn't. Instead, it felt oddly familiar, like a case of déjà vu. If what everyone had told me was true, it was familiar; I had been here before. This had been my home at some point.

I hope they're okay. Lily. Wolfe. Callan. My pack. I'd barely met them, and yet, it was like I'd finally found a place I belonged. At least, it had been until I learned I was a halfling Faerie shifter with lightning powers, the daughter of a bloodthirsty queen. And again, I found myself on the outside. I had so many questions still left unanswered, especially for Callan and his redheaded psycho *mate*.

I shuddered against the thought, snapping my emotional walls back into place as I turned back toward land. I didn't have time to digest anything that had happened in the last few hours, and I especially didn't have time to dwell on the panther shifter that always seemed to make my heart beat faster. Not when I had been dropped into the Faerie realm by myself, completely unarmed if you didn't count the unreliable powers I didn't know how to use and this shifting I had a hard time triggering. My best bet was to regroup with Oliver as soon as possible. Had he even made it out?

I started walking, needing to find some sort of shelter but knowing I shouldn't stray too far. Oliver said he would find me, and while I still didn't know if I could trust him or if he was even still alive, I didn't have much of a choice. This world was already so unlike my own, and I had no idea what else was in store. What if there was acid rain that fell at a moment's notice? Or giant monsters that liked to eat little rabbit shifters? I would be royally screwed.

I'd wait and hope I didn't come to regret that decision.

As I continued, a large outcropping of rocks swam into view, and I picked up my pace as I eyed the darkening sky. I didn't know what nightfall was like out here or even if it worked the same as it did back home, but I'd rather be under cover than out in the open like I was now.

My haste was rewarded when, a few minutes later, I reached the rocks. It was an impressive formation, the large shapes jutting out in all directions, almost throne-like in their pattern. It towered over me, and I sighed in relief when I noticed a small alcove formed in the base of the rocks. It was big enough that I could sit comfortably, and I plopped down, stretching my legs out in front of me as I prepared to wait.

I thought back to the loud blasts I'd heard from Oliver's end of the portal and truly contemplated if he had survived or not. If he was dead, and I was just sitting here like bait, then I might as well drown myself in the strange ocean now. It was probably Queen Tantaii, busting out from the rubble that had been dropped on her. I know they said Oliver was powerful, but was he powerful enough to go up against a Faerie queen? I had my doubts. But what else could I do? I resolved to wait just for the night, and if he hadn't found me by morning, then I'd venture out on my own. I needed food and water. I was no use to anyone if I was dead.

My thoughts returned to Queen Tantaii. Formerly trapped queen of the Fae. *Mother*?

I frowned, my heart rate quickening as my emotions came rushing in, the information of what I had learned fully sinking in. I was half-Fae, and my mother was the queen of the fucking Fae. It was hard to deny that she wasn't just an older, more ethereal version of my own reflection with how similar we looked. Same blonde hair, same big brown eyes. A normal person would probably be happy about that, but this was anything but normal.

3

What had she done that was so bad she was magically locked up for five hundred years?

Olette. A version of myself that I'd chosen to forget. A version I didn't know. I couldn't imagine a world where I'd ever voluntarily give up my memories, not in a billion years. Memories were like my favorite trashy reality TV show—I needed them, no matter how embarrassing or cringe-worthy they might be.

And I needed them back now.

Where the hell is Oliver? The longer I sat there, the wider the pit of dread in my stomach grew. He should have been here by now.

"*Screeeee—*"

My head whipped up, and I stared out of my alcove, cautiously moving into a kneeling position. I listened intently, until I heard the cry again. A high-pitched screech, but soft, like a baby animal.

"*Screeeeee!*"

It was louder this time, almost pained, and I cautiously exited the cave. I followed the continuing cries until I came up to a small rock ledge near the opposite side, where a small figure tossed and turned.

I stared at the strange animal. It was unlike anything I'd ever seen before, like a cross between an eagle and a chicken. It was completely white, with feathered wings protruding from its torso and tucked tightly into its back. The only spot of color on it was its crimson eyes, currently scrunched in pain as it contorted on the ledge. A metal-tipped arrow stuck out of its hind leg, and I softened in sympathy for the creature.

I approached the cheagle, careful to keep my hands out where it could see them. "Easy there, buddy. I'm just going to take a look and see if I can help you out, okay?"

Close enough now, I could see *it* was definitely a *he*. He focused one eye on me as he cried, his screams dying down into a soft, mewling sound that made my heart wrench. I met his gaze, doing my best to give him a reassuring smile. He growled softly as

I got closer, and when I reached one hand out to touch him, he swiped at me with his good leg, a deep slice opening on my hand.

"OW!" I shrieked, pulling my hand back and giving him the evil eye. "Do you want me to help you or not?" He quieted and regarded me, and for a split second, I thought he almost looked human, but then he whimpered and pushed his injured leg out towards me.

"I don't think I should pull it out," I mused to myself. His leg was as white as the rest of him, stained with a shimmery liquid that oozed from the wound. *Silver blood*? "It's better to leave it in so you don't bleed out until we can—" What? Call for help? Get to a hospital? I had no way to help this creature.

The cheagle made a noise deep in his chest, and I squinted at him. He blinked at me expectantly, and I shook my head, incredulous. "You want me to take this out?" He let out a soft chirp, sounding weak. This baby animal understood what I was saying. What kind of place was this?

I assessed the damage, becoming more hopeful as I looked on. The arrow was thinner than it had appeared, lightweight and tipped at both ends with a silvery gray metal that had gone straight through his thigh. Luckily, the body of the arrow was wood, and the arrow was off to the side, hopefully missing any major arteries. If the animals in this realm even had arteries.

"This is going to hurt," I told him as I positioned my hands at one end of the arrow. A trickle of my blood dripped off my wrist, still leaking from the cut he'd made but already starting to itch, a sign my shifter healing was kicking in. I was relieved to know it still worked the same in this realm.

He closed his eyes, and I saw his sturdy chest expand as he took a deep breath. I didn't hesitate, gripping the arrow between my fists and wrenching my hands in different directions, breaking the arrow with only a little resistance. The cheagle shrieked in pain, but I powered through, yanking both ends of the arrow out of their respective spots. His shriek intensified before dying out into complete silence. I glanced at his prone form. He'd passed out from the pain, his chest still rising and falling steadily. *Poor baby.*

I stared at the wound, watching as the skin slowly started to knit itself back together. Now I understood why he'd wanted me to take it out; he healed just like I did. I stood there, not quite sure what to do with myself. I looked around in the blue haze of the landscape, but there was no sign of any other life. Where had this little thing come from? And who had put this arrow in it?

It seemed to have gotten as dark as it was going to, the dual moons still casting enough light to be able to move around, but not a good idea to travel in. The temperature had dropped, and I shivered lightly, missing my usual leather jacket. I eyed the creature, not wanting to leave him out here where he could be seen as easy prey to any passersby.

"You better not wake up and decide I'm the enemy," I muttered under my breath, gingerly cradling him in my arms and lifting him up. While I could probably take him, I didn't want to deal with those razor-sharp claws. He wasn't much bigger than a toddler, but he was dense, my arms dipping with the effort of carrying him. We retreated to my cave, and I gently laid him down in one corner, taking the opposite for myself. It was a tight squeeze, but he radiated a surprising amount of heat, and I found myself huddling closer to him. The wound on his leg was already healed, as was the cut on my hand, the dried crust of blood the only evidence of any injury at all.

I sat propped up with my back against the wall, doing my best to stay awake and stand guard until morning, but exhaustion dragged at me, tugging at the corners of my resolve until I was a lost cause. Between the quiet peacefulness of the world outside and the rhythmic breaths of the cheagle next to me, I faded into blissful oblivion.

CHAPTER TWO

It was the scream that woke me up.

At least, I thought it was a scream until I opened my eyes and saw the baby cheagle, his little body practically vibrating with bristled energy, high-pitched screeches coming from his maw. The wounded animal I had seen the night before was nowhere to be seen. My body seized in fear as I came face to face with what he was shrieking at.

A gargantuan creature blocked the entrance to our shelter. It stood a few heads taller than the cave mouth but had no trouble pinning me with its crimson stare. I couldn't see its wings, but the hulking shoulders told me everything I needed to know. This was not an animal to be fucked with. Its body was a mirror image of my unlikely companion, except where his feathers were white and pristine, this one's were in various hues of blue and green. Long, deadly claws adorned its feet, and I swallowed. Hard. I'd *definitely* die if grabbed by one of those. Its head dipped down toward me until we were level before it opened its pointed beak, a sharp, menacing squawk bursting out.

This was mommy cheagle, and she was *mad*.

I scrambled backward, my back thudding against the wall as I tried not to shit my pants in fear. Baby cheagle moved to stand in

front of me, again screeching at its mother. Defending me, I realized. My heart would have warmed if I wasn't a few feet away
from my imminent death.

Mommy cheagle huffed as she angled her head downward,
locking eyes with me.

'My kin tells me you helped him.' A gasp escaped me as she
spoke into my mind. Her voice was surprisingly soft for how
menacing she looked, yet strong and mature. There was a heavi-
ness to her words, and it was almost too much for my mind to
withstand, a dull ache setting in as I tried to adjust. It was nothing
like when we had talked to each other in animal form back at the
Clover pack. This was something different, something ancient.
She waited for me to respond, but I just gaped my mouth open
like a fish, struggling under the weight of her presence. *'You are
not smart,'* she observed, her disdain blatant.

I cleared my throat, snapping my jaw shut and giving my head
a quick shake. *Get your shit together.* "I didn't do much; just
pulled the arrow out of his leg." The gratitude at my voice not
wavering was immense. Defending my intelligence to this creature
didn't seem like a smart move.

*'He lives because of your actions. And for that, I owe you a
debt.'* Sunlight glinted off her feathers, casting a crystalline glow
throughout the cave. Her gaze was sincere, her head bowed, and
the edges of my fear faded, replaced with a blanket of awe at the
magnificent creature. *'That was an arrow forged by iron, which is
toxic and deadly to most Faerie kind. But if you ever lay a hand on
another pagu, I will hook my talon in your throat and eviscerate
you.'* The terror flooded back, and I nodded in understanding.
Pagu, not cheagle. No touchy. Got it.

'Come. Stop cowering on the ground.' I scooted out and up as
she backed away from the entrance, still careful to keep a
watchful eye in case I needed to run. It seemed like we had some
weird sort of truce, but she'd also just threatened my life, and I
couldn't be too careful. Now, on my feet, I could see she was
easily a few feet taller than me. Her wings were pulled into her

back, her chest jutting forward proudly as she stood, eyeing my meager stature.

'I would have thought a princess would be more . . . impressive.' I tensed at her words, eyes wide.

"You know who I am?"

The beast snorted, light whisps of smoke escaping her. *'There are only three Fae that I know of with hair like that.'* I frowned at her, my hands coming up to smooth my golden tresses down. It'd been a while since I'd seen a brush, but I didn't think it was that bad. Then I thought back to what I've seen. Cas and Queen Tantaii, and their hair that mirrored my own.

"We are the only ones that have blonde hair?"

The pagu's eyes narrowed as she scanned me up and down critically. Judgment and anger lurked in their depth. I didn't know how, but she knew what I had done. She knew I'd forgotten. *'When you live as long as we do, knowledge is the universe's greatest gift. To squander that is a death sentence.'*

"I had a good reason." My response was defensive, but when being accused by a mythical flying creature, it was bound to happen. "You don't know what you're talking about." I cringed as soon as I said it. Not only would upsetting this creature likely get me killed, but *I* didn't even know what I was talking about. I was still trying to wrap my head around how my past self could have made such a decision. Probably the same way I always made decisions: without *thinking first.*

She snorted, shuffling restlessly where she stood. *'Why are you here?'*

"Well . . . It all started when I was kidnapped by a rude ass cu—"

'I do not care, halfling. Why are you sleeping on this beach? This is pagu territory. I would normally skin any trespassers who dared to enter and feed their flesh to my children.'

My breathing wavered, but I steeled myself, doing my best to remind myself that if she wanted to kill me, she would have by now. *Just keep telling yourself that.* "I'm looking for my companion. We were separated when he opened a portal for me to this realm, but he was attacked before he could follow me through."

I looked out toward the sea, the sun sitting low on the horizon as it rose, casting a brilliant golden pathway across the water's surface. Its shimmer, combined with the red of the water, made it look like a thousand tiny flames dancing, painting the sea in an impressive display of fiery hues that stretched on forever.

"I was hoping he'd show up by morning." My words were soft, resigned to what had probably happened. Oliver hadn't made it, and now I was stuck here alone. Panic started to seep in, weaving its way around my fragile walls like a serpent coiling to strike.

'I will help you, and the debt will be paid.' I thought about refusing, still not entirely sure this animal didn't still want to kill me. But what other choice did I have? I needed to find Oliver. I needed food, water, and shelter. I needed her help.

"Thank you. Do you have a name? What can I call you? I'm Rowan."

'The closest translation to your language would be Aura. He has not earned his name yet.' She turned to the baby, who had been watching us silently for the past few minutes. After a few seconds of chattering between the two that sounded suspiciously like an argument, he approached me, coming to a stop before me. He stared at me expectantly, his red eyes looking as innocent as possible, and I chided myself for being afraid of the small animal.

I stooped down, closer to his height, and craned my neck toward him. I'm not sure what he wanted, but he'd also saved me from getting eaten, so a little trust was warranted. He lightly laid his beak on my arm, meeting my eyes, and I melted. He was thanking me. "You're welcome, little dude," I said as I cautiously reached out, giving his head a small pat.

'Go back to the stronghold.' Aura glared at him until he hunched his shoulders for a moment before his wings shot out, and he launched himself into the air unsteadily. With a few surges, he was airborne, flying off into the distance, wavering slightly back

and forth in the air as he went until he was just a small speck in the distance.

'Let us go; I believe I know where your friend is. If I am right, we need to get there sooner than later. Normally, I would only let my Marked rider on my back, but I will make an exception this time.'

"Did you just say *rider*?"

The rocky terrain underneath us shifted slightly as Aura bent down, her legs folding underneath themselves until she resembled a chicken sitting on her eggs. Except there were no eggs, only a very pointed look she was giving me that I really didn't want to see.

'Get on. Try anything funny, and I'll slit your throat.'

CHAPTER THREE

R iding a pagu was *not* easy.

Not that it had seemed easy in the first place.

After three tries, I finally managed to hoist myself onto Aura's back. Her feathers were surprisingly sturdy, providing ample purchase for me to use my feet as leverage to get on. The only handholds available were the two protruding horns that I discovered on the back of her neck, so I used those to steady myself as I cinched my knees to her sides. One wrong move and I'd slide off. My grip on her horns would be the only thing holding me to her. My sweaty, sweaty grip.

"I think I'm going to die?" It came out as a question, unable to hide the high-pitched nervousness in my voice.

The chances of you falling off are slim.' That did nothing to reassure me. My fingers gripped tighter around her horns, my knuckles turning white.

"But not zero?" I had a hard enough time getting on a roller coaster without getting nauseous. A flying Faerie creature? I was definitely dying.

'Never zero.' The seriousness in her tone ate up any remnants of confidence I had left. Maybe we could just walk instead. *'But*

my magic will hold you in place once we fly. As long as I have the energy for it, you will stay seated.' Sweat beaded on my brow, but I tightened my grip around the horns I held, hardening the walls of my shaky heart. I could do this.

"So how does this—" The breath was stolen from my lungs, the air rushing past us as we launched into the sky, a jump so high it had to have been aided by magic. An immediate iron-clad sensation locked my legs to her side, unable to move them even if I wanted to, but I still gripped her horns as Aura's wings flapped hard in the air as we rose above the rocky dunes below. It wasn't long before she was high in the sky, and we settled into a steady rhythm, soaring steadily toward an outcropping of trees in the distance.

I stared in awe as we crested the forest, this world so unlike the one I had come from, different yet entirely similar. They looked like trees, but the colors were off. Where brown bark should have stood, instead, they were a deep ebony with leafy, pumpkin-dusted branches. *Weird.*

"How do we find him?" I half shouted to Aura, not sure if she would be able to hear me around the wind. "I don't even know if he's here. He could be dead." Dread settled in my stomach at the thought. I didn't want to know what would happen to me if Oliver was dead.

'Pagu are connected to the magic that runs through the veins of this realm more than any other creature. We are born of this land. Its protectors, once upon a time.' Her tone was that of a teacher who had to explain something to a child for the tenth time, clear irritation laced throughout. She banked to the right as we approached, the land stretching endlessly beneath us. I hazarded a glance behind us. The salty air of the sea long faded for the earthiness of our new surroundings. *'Portals use a lot of energy, something I can sense throughout the realm. I felt one when you came through, and it led me to you as I searched for my kin. But I felt another, deep into the night.'*

A flutter of hope bloomed in my chest at her words. I didn't trust Oliver, not fully, but so far he hadn't led me astray. He was the only one who could hopefully give me some answers and lead me back to my memories. According to him, the survival of the realms depended on it. Whatever that was supposed to mean.

But if Oliver had come last night, then why hadn't he found me? Unease shivered through me as my mind raced with the many possible outcomes.

Aura dipped lower in the sky as we approached a large clearing in the woods, and I clenched my grip tight on her horns even though my legs stayed secured by her magic. She stilled, hovering inches above the trees as she peered down into the clearing. Her wings barely moved, just enough to keep us afloat but not so much as to attract any unwanted attention as she cocked her head, listening.

"What do you—" I started in a whisper when I couldn't wait any longer, but I was quickly silenced when I heard the hissing. It was faint, almost imperceptible, but the whimper that followed wasn't. It was heartbreakingly familiar.

Oliver.

Aura tensed underneath me, every muscle in her body coiling tightly. *'Be prepared.'*

I craned my neck to the side, shifting so I could see down into the clearing, but I didn't have time before she tucked her wings tight against her flank, nosediving toward the ground at rapid speed. I gasped as we hurtled downward, my stomach hitting rock bottom as she bottomed out, wings shooting out at the last second to halt her descent. I looked around the clearing, beads of sweat slithering down my back when I saw the creatures that surrounded Oliver. I couldn't see his face, but he was unmoving, bent over, and bleeding on the ground.

Five enemies surrounded him, and I wasn't sure if I should call them human or animal. They stood tall, all covered with the same green, leathery skin. Identical dark hair was braided down their backs, their bodies clad in a shimmering silver armor that fit like a glove. They looked almost normal if it wasn't for their faces.

A narrow, flattened head housed large soulless eyes with slit pupils, a stark contrast to their mouths, which were gaping open in an aggressive hinge. It provided a full view of their sharp fangs and forked tongues. At our arrival, they turned their attention away from their prey, the sleek daggers they held coming up to point at us. A swirling black-green sludge coated the blades, wrapped threateningly around the steel.

'*Go to your friend,*' Aura told me seriously. The magic around my legs released, and I haphazardly slid back to the ground, my boots landing on the dirt with a muted thud. '*I can handle them. The day I let a naga best me in a fight is the day I deserve to die. Stay out of my way.*'

I started to argue until the naga took a collective step toward us, spreading out into a menacing half-moon of imminent death. I inched backward, not sure how I was supposed to get to Oliver without also getting impaled on a snake man's blade. The closest one on my right saw my hesitation, and he launched forward with a strangled hiss, dagger held out in front of him to attack. I had a brief second to panic before a giant feathered wing smacked into my side, launching me off to the side in a crumpled heap in the dirt.

Aura used the distraction to her advantage, launching into the air toward the green bastard with her razor-like talons. She speared him clean through, easily a head and shoulders above his height, his body stuck on her menacing knives. She flapped her wings hard, launching a few feet into the air. The muscles in her legs bunched together as she tensed, and a disgusting, wet, ripping sound had my gut churning as she tore him in half, his innards splattering the ground. She shook off her feet for a brief second before she launched herself at the next one. The naga had completely forgotten about me and all rushed to attack the enraged pagu while she cut them down one by one with savage precision. I took advantage of the chaos, hustling over to where Oliver's prone form lay.

The Fae was in bad shape, his clothes in tatters and small slices all over his skin, the edges oozing a disgusting dark sludge. His chest rose and fell erratically, and his skin shone, slick with sweat, as a fever raged inside him. Those knives were coated in poison, without a doubt.

"What do I do?" I muttered to no one, not sure where to even begin helping him. I looked behind me to see Aura was almost finished with her battle, her feathers soaked in crimson blood. She was incredible, equal parts vicious and deadly. Another reminder to never get on her bad side.

"*Rowan,*" Oliver wheezed, snapping my attention back to him as relief poured into me at seeing him awake. His eyelids fluttered as he struggled to remain conscious, a slight moan coming from deep in his chest.

"Those knives are poisoned, aren't they? Do you have an antidote?" I slapped his cheek lightly as he started to drift off, hoping I could get enough information from him that would save his life. I didn't know if Fae healed the same way shifters do, but it sure didn't seem like it.

He met my glance for a second with glassy eyes before they rolled back, a seizure taking over his body, violent and sudden.

'Turn him on his side,' Aura commanded, coming to a soft land next to me. I quickly gripped his arm and pulled, heaving him onto one side with a grunt of effort. We were right on time, and a few seconds later, he vomited on the floor.

"What do we do?" I asked her, concern eating away at me.

'Naga venom is deadly, killing those infected within hours. They mix it on their blades with iron dust, a deadly combination. Normally, we'd use an anti-venom, but in a pinch, it can be cured directly from the naga. By eating a fresh heart. Go get one.'

Gross. No shortage of those here.

I stood, running over to the gruesome remains of what used to be our attackers, homing in on one whose guts were spilling from a gaping hole that opened from his throat to his navel. Nausea pulled at me, and I swallowed, hoping I could get the heart and save Oliver without puking my guts out.

The knees of my jeans squelched in blood as I kneeled in front of the body, plunging my hand into the chest cavity before I could think too much about what I was doing. The naga anatomy was surprisingly familiar, helping me to locate the heart with no problem. Aura's claws had done a number, the ribcage easily separating under my frantic guidance. I wrapped my hand around the heart, which came away with little resistance. Bile rose in my throat as I tried to think of anything but what I was currently holding. It was small enough that I could hold it in one hand, but I cupped it in both anyways, the slippery texture unsteady against my skin as I carried it back to Oliver, now still but breathing.

I stared from him to the heart. If I just put the whole thing in his mouth and he didn't chew, he was going to choke, and that wouldn't help this situation at all.

'Squeeze it into his mouth. That should be enough for now until we can get him to our healers.' Aura watched my struggle with impatience. 'Hurry. We need to move before more of them come.'

I winced as I held the heart over his mouth, using one hand to hold it open. My fingers tightened as hard as I could, and I gagged at the feeling of the heart bursting underneath my fingertips but held steady as the rivulets of blood dripped into his mouth. Chunks of meat and gore pooled in his throat, and I breathed a sigh of relief when he swallowed on reflex. Immediately, the sludge oozing from his wounds started to slow.

'That's enough,' Aura called to me, shifting down until her head was bowed in front of me in invitation. 'He will live. I will take you to my home, and after that, you must leave.'

I wasn't going to argue with the killing machine, so I mounted her after a few moments of struggle, relaxing my hold a little when I felt her magic grip me into place. I looked at my comatose companion lying on the ground, pink already starting to come back to his cheeks. There was no way he would fit on her back with me, not like that. "What about Oliver?"

'I will carry him, of course.' She surged into the air, hovering over him with her mighty talons. I thought they were just for stabbing, but she impressed me with her agility as she cradled him gently between them instead, the claws long enough to carry the unconscious man. *'Try not to annoy me. It's a three-hour flight.'*

CHAPTER FOUR

One thing they don't tell you about flying is how freaking *cold* it was.

By the time we landed in the pagu's village, my teeth were chattering, and I was pretty sure my eyes were only still open because they had frozen that way. Their dwelling wasn't what I had expected. Well, not that I was really sure what type of house a giant murderous bird would live in, but I was thinking of a tree. Or a nest built off the skulls of their enemies.

Instead, they lived surrounded by cliffs and steep drop-offs. An entire village existed, filled with modest stone huts and aged structures. There were plenty of pagu that roamed about, but much to my surprise, people milled about too. Most of them were tall and slim, with elongated ears and striking features I'd come to recognize as Fae. Some of them bore striking black tattoos, stretching over their exposed skin like midnight spiderwebs. All eyes turned to me, whispers breaking out as we dropped in front of a larger open-faced hut with cots, vials, and a cauldron off to one side. It was like a witchy hospital.

A harried-looking Fae with blue hair popped out, running to meet Oliver, where he was unceremoniously dropped on the floor by Aura when we landed. I was bent over him, and she nudged me over hard enough to knock me over.

"Move," she ordered—completely unnecessarily, given she'd moved me herself. She held her hands out in front of her, hovering over Oliver's body.

"What are you doing?" I questioned, but she didn't respond, her entire being focused on the man in front of her.

'She's helping him,' Aura said, and by the way the girl's eyes darted up, I realized she could hear her too. *'Pulling the remaining poison out will help him heal much faster than waiting for the medicine of the naga heart to work its way completely through him.'*

The girl swirled her hands in front of her, and I watched in awe as the green sludge that still coated Oliver's wounds started to shake and then rise. More green essence floated out, Oliver giving a weak whimper as the poison was magically pulled from the gashes. After a few silent moments, no more poison escaped, and she urged the floating putrid ball into a small pouch she held at her hip.

"He'll be fine in a few hours. Great thinking with the heart, Aura." She nodded tersely to the pagu as she stood, a movement of begrudging respect. She grinned suddenly, her cobalt hair cascading like a waterfall down her back. She was pretty, in a scary, don't-fuck-with-me kind of way. "And now I have a healthy resupply of naga venom for our next raid."

"Raid?" I asked her, unable to stop myself. She looked me up and down, her monolid eyes focusing on me for the first time since I'd arrived. They lingered on my hair, and remembering what Aura had told me earlier, I knew it was because of the color.

'Nia, this is Rowan. Nia is my Marked. And a water user.'

"Marked?"

'A special set of Fae are born with an enhanced connection to the magic of the realm. They are born with twisting ebony art on their skin. When they are old enough, we bond with them, and they help us to do our jobs of protecting the realm.'

I looked between the two of them, and honestly, it made

sense. I hadn't known Nia long, but she clearly was used to being in charge and getting her way, and I'd learned from experience that Aura was the same. Did all riders match their pagu's personality, or was it just a coincidence?

"You are a lightning wielder." The hardness in her expression was jarring, but I straightened my posture, not one to wither under a hostile stare that I met confidently. She hadn't asked me a question, so I remained silent. Finally, she broke eye contact and pivoted to face Aura, careful not to turn her back completely to me. She waved her hands wildly, and Aura shifted uncomfortably, ruffling her wings every now and again. It was very clear they were having a conversation about me that I couldn't hear.

I made a mental note to figure out exactly how this communication thing worked. And how everything worked, while we were at it. I had finally been getting to a place back at the Clover pack where I felt like I understood everything that was going on, but now here I was again, dropped into a world I didn't understand. Again.

An angry outburst from Aura broke me out of my thoughts, and Nia turned back toward me, every bit the scolded child. Begrudgingly, she said, "I apologize for my behavior. Your kin and I have a lot of bad blood."

"I don't remember them. I don't remember any of my time in this realm," I told her honestly. I was again faced with someone I had no reason to trust, but I wanted Nia to like me. I'd come to like Aura, even though I knew she was seconds away from cutting my head off at any moment. I didn't truly believe she would, given how much she had helped me so far. If Nia was her rider, then there had to be a redeeming quality in there somewhere. "That's why I'm here. The Queen has been freed. I don't know what she wants, but I know that I need to get my memories back as soon as possible. Somehow."

Nia paled, a dark look passing over her face as realization hit her. "You're the princess, aren't you?"

That was the second time someone had called me that, and I

winced at the name, not feeling the least bit princess *anything*. Just because all these other people knew who I was didn't mean that I did. "Don't call me that. My name is Rowan. Whoever I was before, or who you think I was, isn't me anymore."

"Let's get your friend inside and get you cleaned up," Nia told me with a pointed look at my sordid outfit. She waved her hands again like she was molding the air, and Oliver floated a few feet above the ground. My mouth hung open as I watched her effortlessly guide Oliver to a meager hut toward one side of the village. A sly look spread across her face at my confusion. "Fun fact: Fae are mostly water. Well, water and magic. When we die, we just put our bodies in the crimson ocean to become one again. I'm not the best at it, but I can throw a few bodies around when I need to."

Wow. Remind me not to get on her bad side.

I expected Aura to follow, but instead, she launched into the sky, flying off toward a higher cliff that I bet was where the pagu lived. I stared down at my hands as we walked, remembering the feeling of utter power I had been able to wield before. Remembering the torture from Lexi and the betrayal of Cas, who I had thought I could trust, ignited my anger, little zaps of energy prickling off my fingertips in every direction. Nia looked down, a smirk spreading across her shapely lips. "Careful with those. I remember what my powers were like when I didn't know how to control them."

I bit back the retort I had prepped on my tongue. She was right. I had no idea what I was doing on either side of my heritage. I had little control over my lightning, and I couldn't shift into my rabbit form for shit. I was useless. I took a calming breath, dropping my hands back down to my sides.

We made it to the hut, and with a little maneuvering, Nia was able to float Oliver through, landing him gently on the only bed in the room. It was modestly decorated, with a small sink and toilet in one corner and a rickety bookshelf stocked with strange-looking leather-bound texts the only other furniture. Oliver was already starting to look better, his breathing now coming in deep, steady intervals as he slept.

"What is this place?" I asked Nia as we took a seat at the table. Her observant gaze watched me like a hawk. I didn't think many things got past her scrutiny.

"The Briar Stronghold. Pagu and their riders didn't used to live in hiding. There was a time when riders ruled the realm centuries ago. Pagu are born from the magic that flows through the Faerie realm, the original Faerie, and together with their riders they are dutybound to make sure it stays alive."

"Stays alive? I thought magic was limitless?"

Nia laughed, a cold, bitter sound. When she answered, I could see the pain etched on her face, something she tried to keep hidden and couldn't. "The magic in this realm is dying, Rowan. Queen Tantaii has been siphoning it for centuries for her own selfish gain. We got lucky when they cursed her away and halted her progress, but her magic went with her. The magic won't recover, not until she's dead. And even then, who knows how much damage she's already done. It's like she opened a wound, and each year, the magic dwindles a little bit more."

My heart broke at the anguish in her voice. Nia cared deeply for this world. Her world. How could a ruler feed on their kingdom to the point that it could destroy it? What kind of selfish person did that, and for what reason besides power? "Why didn't they kill her?"

"No one knows." She shrugged. "It was a very long time ago. Fae are living shorter and shorter lives with our magic dwindling, and not many of us were alive to see her imprisonment. Thrones are won by combat. After she was cursed, Casimir claimed the throne. He's her—"

"I know who he is," I interrupted. If you'd asked me a month ago, I would have said Chad, my cheating ex-boyfriend, was at the top of my shit list, but now it was definitely Cas. At this point, I needed to start a running list of who I wanted to kill. Ruby, Lexi, Cas, and Queen Tantaii, in no particular order.

"Right. Of course you do." Her gaze drifted up toward my hair again, and I smoothed down my golden locks self-consciously. I used to like the color of my hair, but now it felt like something I should be ashamed of. "His rule is all I've ever known. He's been challenged many times, but he remains the strongest. He is smart enough not to siphon any more magic, but he's not a ruler. He's a tyrant. He doesn't care about restoring the realm, he only cares about power. He's been searching for a way to free Queen Tantaii for centuries. And now he has. With her free . . . I don't know what the future holds for the realm, but it isn't good."

I looked down at my hands, anxiety coursing through me as I picked at my fingernail beds. This was all my fault. I'd played right into their hands and went along with their spell like a stupid fucking idiot. They'd put me in a tough spot by threatening the lives of my friends, but was that really worth the lives of everyone in this realm? My heart said I'd made the right choice, but my head didn't.

"I'm the reason she's free," I told Nia, my head still bowed. I clenched my eyes shut, afraid to see her reaction, as I told her I was the reason her world was going to end. "I didn't know. I must have thought going to the shifter realm would be enough to hide, but they found me. And they used me to set her free."

Nia was silent for so long I thought she might have left, and I chanced a glance upward. Her eyes were filled with rage, the dark pools of midnight lit by a fire within, but she didn't scream or yell at me like I expected her to. If anything, her silence was worse.

I forced myself not to look away. Dominance contests must not work between Fae as I felt no urge to look away besides my own shame, which I was grateful for. The last thing I needed was for this Fae to also hate me because I challenged her to something that I wasn't sure I would win.

Finally, she breathed deeply, closing her eyes as she let her anger ride out with her exhale.

"You didn't know," she said evenly. Her diplomacy impressed

me. I knew I wouldn't have been able to be so understanding if our roles were reversed. "I can question your judgment, but I cannot fault you for what you didn't know. But you need to help us fix this. For good."

My palpable relief surprised me as I nodded my agreement. I normally didn't care what others thought of me, but Nia was strong, clearly some sort of leader in this place. If all she said was true, then my journey was far from over. If the only way out of this was to kill the Queen, then I needed all the allies I could get. I felt responsible for this.

I mulled over what I had learned, questions tugging at my mind. "What I don't understand is why the traitor would put her in the ground, not kill her, and then leave the throne open for Cas to claim. And why did they need me to break her out?"

Nia opened her mouth to respond, but it was a weak voice from the bed that drew my attention instead. "Because it was you. You cursed her underground, and then you abandoned your duty and ran."

Oliver was awake.

The look of shock on my face was a direct mirror to the one Nia wore. Oliver said nothing further, gingerly pulling himself up into a sitting position. His eyes were clear and strong, the dark circles beneath them the only giveaway that he had been inches away from death's doorstep.

"I wouldn't. . ." But I trailed off. I didn't know what I would have done. I'd like to think I was still the same person now that I was then, but how could I be when I couldn't remember the life experiences that made me who I was? All I had were the memories in my head now of a childhood where I wasn't wanted and a slew of bad decisions. Where did the real memories begin and the fake memories end? "How long have I been in the human realm, Oliver?"

"One hundred years, give or take. Fae age incredibly slowly. Think millennia." I searched his face for any sign of deception, or maybe a smile and a laugh to say he was joking, but it didn't come.

Sweat slicked my palms, a nervous tingle settling into the soles of my feet as I digested that information.

"A hundred years? I don't understand. I—I remember everything. The foster homes, the schools, the boyfriends. I remember it all." I stopped talking, not because I didn't have more to say, but because I could no longer breathe normally, the air coming out of me in short, urgent gasps as the panic attack came on.

I couldn't wrap my mind around it. A hundred years is an incredibly long time. There was no way I was out there in the human realm, restarting my life every . . . what, ten years? Twenty? Over and over and over again. And I didn't remember any of it. I never had any inkling that something was amiss, not until that night after the car wreck when Lexi bit me.

If I wasn't already sitting, I probably would have fallen.

"Breathe," Nia urged me. I'm not sure when she had moved, but now she crouched in front of me. She set her hands on my shoulders, and a cold chill flooded through my body, freezing the ball of anxiety inside of me. She kept her hands where they were, and after a few moments, I calmed, doing my best to breathe deeply. Oliver watched us from his bed, expressionless.

"I will tell you everything, Rowan, but you have to listen," he said finally. In his Fae form, he didn't look much older than forty, his pointed ears peeking out of the top of his silver hair. It would take some getting used to his appearance from the witch façade of the old man I had originally known him as. "You asked why you ran? Because that's what you always do. Your first instinct is to always run, it always has been. And like I've been telling you for five hundred years, you cannot run from this. Not anymore."

He pulled himself out of the bed slowly until he stood on two feet. He swayed slightly, and Nia rushed over to steady him, her frosty healing leaving me feeling empty but calm. I saw the same tranquility spread into Oliver, and he stood straighter almost immediately.

"You shouldn't be up. Your body will recover at double the rate if you sleep."

"I'll be okay, dear. This is important. The sooner we are all on the same page, the better," he said, gently patting her hand before removing it. He took a breath as her power withdrew from him, but still, he remained steady. A loud rumble echoed in the small hut, and he gave a sheepish grin, a little bit of the cheery light I had seen before returning to his eyes. "Food first, yes?"

CHAPTER FIVE

The eating area of the Briar Stronghold was impressive.
Where the houses were plain and modest, the eating hut
was anything but. It was similarly made of stone like the
housing, but there was no roof. Instead, the room was tall and
wide with long wooden slats laid sparingly over the top for the
pagu to perch on. A large tub of water stood in the middle of the
room, filled with large fish splashing and writhing about as eagle-
eyed pagu peered in from above, occasionally taking a moment to
jump down and get one before flying back up to perch while they
ate their meal.

"We try to keep fish stocked here for them," Nia told me as we
walked in. "When the Queen was cursed, the Marked tried to take
a stand against Casimir, hoping we could right the throne, once
and for all. But he is powerful, almost as powerful as she was, and
his army has only gotten larger. We suffered devastating losses, and
he's been hunting us down ever since. He doesn't want us to ever
have the numbers to challenge him again. The stronghold is
generally safe, but we don't like them venturing too far off the
property. There are hunters specifically tasked with taking us out.
They cannot know about this place."

We stepped up to a small buffet line, and I marveled at the strange food in front of me. There was nothing hot, but instead, many fruits that I recognized but entirely different. Purple bananas, black apples, and blue grapes that were covered completely on the outside by thorns. I could make a whole shopping list out of all the things I saw.

"Only fruit?" I questioned, not that I was complaining. I'd always loved fruit, especially for breakfast. There was just something about the sweetness on your tongue first thing in the morning that really set your day up for success.

"Fae thrive on sweet things, primarily fruit, and don't need much to survive. The magic that runs through this realm runs through us and helps us sustain our life force. And they taste the same." Oliver grinned at me as he grabbed a plate from the side, piling it on with the feast before us. He seemed to be more at ease in this place than I'd ever seen him, despite the attack he'd just endured. I followed suit, grabbing a banana and a grape bunch, vaguely concerned about how I would get around the thorns. I'd bet I could poke someone's eye out with one of those. I left the black apples for another day; there was a limit to how adventurous I could be. "The Faerie realm and the mortal realm are loose reflections of the other, they are tethered together by the magic that lives in both realms. We have a sky with moons and an ocean with water, fruit, and even animals. That is, all the realms are similar but different. Yet they exist in balance."

"So, what happened?" I asked Oliver as we plopped our trays down on a nearby table. "Why didn't you come right through another portal?"

"Tantaii. She burst out of that rubble and did her best to kill me. Portal work takes concentration, and it's very hard to open another portal when a rampaging queen is chasing you. When I was finally able to open one, I didn't have a lot of time to think about where to put it, and I unfortunately spit myself out near a camp of naga. I'm very grateful for your pagu," Oliver said, dipping his head towards Nia in thanks.

She gave him a polite smile in return. She picked a thorny grape off its vine, and I watched as she pulled the fruit apart by the thorns, a perfectly round globule plopping onto her plate below before she popped it into her mouth. I did the same thing to one of my own, and I almost moaned as the honeyed sweetness blossomed over my tongue.

"Oh my god, these are amazing!" I exclaimed as I opened a few more, eating through my portion.

Nia crinkled her nose at me, a playful judgment in her eyes as she watched me. "Your gods are inspired by the Fae, by the way."

"How did that happen?" I'd never been much for religion, but I loved a good history lesson.

"People of both realms used to be able to travel freely between the two. It wasn't always that way, but two thousand years ago, the great Fae King Thuromon found a way to open the link. The in-between was just that, a travel stop, with portals always open on both sides. Both realms lived in harmony, in true peace. It really was a beautiful sight." Sadness permeated Oliver's voice.

"What changed?"

"Your mother," Nia offered, a sour expression marring her regal face. "She won a trial by combat challenge against King Thuromon seven hundred years ago, and with his death went the peace. I wish I had been born early enough to see it."

"With the open door between realms, there was a surge of halfling births," Oliver added on. "Shifter halflings are rare given their fertility parameters, but halfling witches, vampires, and even humans ran rampant.

"What exactly is a halfling?" They'd been throwing the term around, but I still didn't quite understand the meaning of it.

"Exactly what it sounds like," he told me. "Born of both a Fae and a being from your realm. Halflings are often very strong, with some of the most powerful beings in our history being of mixed heritage."

"You said vampires? The *Nosferatu* kind or the sparkle-in-the-sunlight bullshit?"

"A little bit of both," Oliver said with a twitch of his lips. A frown split Nia's brow as she looked between the two of us. "I've been around a long time, Rowan. Nearly eight hundred years. Tantaii was always power-hungry—that's never been a question—but she crossed a line after your father."

"You knew my father?" My mind raced with the possibilities. I peeked at Nia, who was silently eating her thorny grapes. She was focused on Oliver, just as curious as I was. "Who was he? Was he . . . a king?" I didn't know exactly how Fae hierarchy worked, but something told me a shifter sitting on the throne of the Fae would be a no-go.

"No, dear. We never met, but I knew of him. I think everyone probably did." His somber tone ate at me, dread filling me as his words hung heavy over my head. I'd never been this close to knowing the truth about my parents, and as much as I didn't think I would like what he had to say, I needed to hear it. I had to. "Tantaii already had a husband when she met your father. King Castiel, Casimir's father. She had an affair. I don't know how long they were together, but shortly after she had you, your father disappeared. No one ever heard from him again."

"He's dead?" My voice was hard to match the walls I had built around my heart. I didn't know this man and would never know him, but that didn't stop the sadness from slithering around, searching for a weakness in the foundation so it could slip its way through and constrict. I refused to let it.

"I assume so. No one has seen him since, and that would be a very long time for a shifter to live. The oldest shifter I've ever met lived to be five hundred before his mind buckled and had to be put down. Their mortal minds just aren't equipped to withstand so much time." Oliver was matter of fact, not like he was telling a child their father was dead and never coming back. "She tracked down as many halflings as she could after that. She killed most of them, even the babies. But she kept a select few."

"Why keep some but not all?"

"Besides the monarch, only halflings can create portals

between the worlds because they are made of magic that runs through both realms. She destroyed the open portals, destroyed anything living that resided in the in-between. It was horrifying. Adults, family members, newborns. She killed them all. Except for a few. Like you and me."

I choked on the bite of banana I was eating, swallowing hard to try and clear it from my throat before I was ready to talk again. Nia saved me from having to talk as she echoed the question in my brain. "You're a halfling too?"

"Yes, half fire-witch. Most witches have a special affinity for something. I believe that's why Tantaii kept me alive. I'm not from a royal family, but my mother was a very powerful fire-witch in the mortal realm. And as you've probably seen, I'm an excellent portal-maker." He only looked slightly cocky as he said it, but I couldn't argue with him. I'd only seen impressive magic from him so far. "She's the reason you had so many magical blocks on you. She was ashamed of you and never wanted you to be a contender for power, but she couldn't bring herself to kill you. So she had your shifter powers sealed at birth instead. It's no wonder you have issues triggering them."

I thumbed another grape in my mouth, the new delicacy still not enough to diminish the dark cloud over my head. Oliver's revelation had me reeling, but it also made sense, and at this moment, I believed him. Rage built inside me at the pain my former self must have gone through. Unwanted. Alone. Powerless.

"What the hell am I supposed to do now?" I asked them, drawing my usual snark to me and welcoming it like an old friend. "She's going to come for her revenge. I know you want me to kill her and all, but I'm sure it's not that easy. I barely even know how to use my abilities."

"She wants more than revenge," Oliver said darkly, his hooded gaze pinned on me, a look of scrutiny in his eyes. "I don't have all the information; I wish that I did. I spent hundreds of years in a cell before you set me free. My life is yours, and I have and will do everything that I can to keep you safe. But you kept a lot of secrets, even from me. As much as she wanted to, the Queen didn't hold the sheer power it would take to destroy the mortal realm on her own. She sought to find the most powerful object in Faerie existence, Oberon's ring, which no one has seen in millennia. The father of all realms. With the ring, he created the realms. And with the ring, they can be taken back."

"Since both realms are intact, she must not have found it. That's good, right?" If the Queen didn't have the ring she needed to destroy the world, then that was in our favor, especially if no one had seen it for thousands of years.

"She didn't find it, but you did. I don't know how you did it, but you used it and cursed her into the ground. It was an ancient curse, one you probably didn't understand fully and could only be lifted with a combination of innocent blood and the free will of the one who put her there." I cringed at his words. I'd completely fallen into their trap to free Tantaii; they'd been playing us the entire time. How could I have been so stupid?

"The Queen liked to punish you in the dungeon beneath the royal castle. She left you there for days, sometimes months at a time. That's where we met. I was the only halfling still left, or so I'd thought." Pain creased his face, making him look older than I'd ever seen him. "After you cursed her, you set me free. You saved my life. I had no one to go back to, so I stayed with you. Against my urging, we ran. For so many years, but Casimir always caught up to us in one way or another. You made the choice to jump into the mortal realm, thinking he wouldn't be able to get to you if there were no halflings left to open a portal."

"Well, that was fucking stupid," I commented, inwardly berating myself. Casimir wasn't a halfling, as far as I knew, so there must have been someone else who allowed them to get through the portal. I should have just killed the Queen. If I had killed her when I had an all-powerful ring and the chance, none of this would have happened. My memories would be intact, and Evie would still be alive. *Evie.* My heart wrenched as I remembered the young girl who would never get to go to a mating party or become a permanent member of the pack. All because of my mistakes.

I blew out a shaky breath, pushing the long-eaten grape carcasses around my plate aimlessly.

"You couldn't let your mother or Casimir ever get their hands on the ring, so we visited the First Goddess, Prim, in the Temple of Primoris. I don't know what was said, but you were with her for days. I was beginning to think she'd killed you for even attempting to visit her; she is not known for her generosity. The night before we were reunited, I dreamt of her. Of Prim. She warned me you would return different and that I was to take you to the mortal realm and never come back. When you finally reemerged, you were no longer Olette. You were Rowan, with a fabricated past already in place, thinking you were eighteen, and I whisked you away through a portal. I followed you around the country, and every ten years like clockwork, your memory reset automatically, and I moved you to a new city every time."

"I never told you where the ring was? Not once in the, what, four hundred years we traveled together?" I wanted to believe that everything he told me was true. He seemed sincere, but I was skeptical. If we'd been companions for so long, I should have learned how to trust him. Why hadn't I?

"No. You said the more I knew, the faster I would die. I stopped asking after the first fifty years." Nia snorted a laugh, and Oliver shot her a sharp glance, but she paid him no mind. If I wasn't so shell-shocked, I might have found it funny. It definitely sounded like something I would say. But instead, my chest was heavy, haunted by the ghosts of my past that I couldn't escape.

I stared around the room without really seeing, lost in thought. As ludicrous as it sounded, I wanted to run. Oliver was right. It was always my first instinct. I'd run when Chad cheated on me. I'd wanted to run when I found out about the Clover pack. And if what Oliver said was true, I ran from . . . everything. My home, my people. I hadn't done what they really needed from me, which was to protect them. I'd left them and had been running for the last five hundred years. The Queen would never stop coming for me, not as long as that ring stayed hidden away from her grasp.

Not only did I have the survival of the Faerie realm on my shoulders, but also the mortal realm. The Clover pack. I had people I cared about, *truly* cared about, and they'd done nothing to deserve what was coming if the Queen got her hands on the ring. Cas knew I cared about them. If he couldn't get what they wanted from me, he'd go for them.

I couldn't let that happen.

"Rowan?" Nia's austere voice penetrated the haze that plagued me, her brows pinched with concern. "Are you alright?"

I stood up from the table, my chair pushing back with a screech at the abrupt move as I stood tall and looked down at them. "No, no, I'm not. I'm angry. I'm confused. I'm hurt." Oliver's surprise was palpable at my words, his mouth dropping open slightly as he watched me. "But more than anything, Nia? I'm *really* fucking exhausted."

"Then what do you want to do?" Oliver asked me, his expression unreadable. He deferred to me, I could see it now. He probably always had. It was why he didn't question me when I wanted to unlock my powers, why he'd never interfered with my decisions thus far. Everything he'd posed to me had been a choice for me to make, to a fault. I wondered if he hadn't stopped asking, would I have eventually told him where the ring was?

"We are going to go see this goddess and get my memories back." I stopped, knowing what I needed to say but not quite sure that I could make the right choice.

"And then?" Oliver prompted me when I didn't continue.

I thought of Evie, taken needlessly. Of Lily and Wolfe and the light they'd brought into my life in the short time I'd known them. Of Callan, who was equal parts enticing and infuriating at the same time. And of Nia and the pagu, who I'd only just met but already had shown me some of the magic and strife that consumed my home realm. Both realms depended on me.

No, this wasn't a choice. I was done running.

I had to be.

"And then we kill my mother."

CHAPTER SIX

"**W**hy do you wear these pants? This dunam?" Nia asked me as we stood in the armory of the Briar Stronghold. Oliver said he had some things to procure for our journey and had flown away on a cranky Aura a few hours ago. I was shocked she hadn't dumped him on his ass the second he mounted up, but Nia had called in a special favor. If I wasn't mistaken, it seemed the protective bird had a soft spot for the old halfling witch.

The armory was surprisingly impressive, a vast room with floor-to-ceiling racks filled with more weapons than I could even name, all consisting of the sharp and pointy kind. In the center were large wicker baskets, filled to the brim with clothing stacked in neatly folded piles.

"Denim," I corrected her. "We call them jeans in the mortal realm. You don't have anything like that here?"

"Why would we wear something so impractical? And tight?" She scoffed at my suggestion, and I eyed the simple ensemble she wore, a tight-fitting tunic that highlighted her battle-harden muscles paired with a simple pair of black breeches. I still wore my ratty jeans, stiff with crusted dirt and other things I didn't want to identify. "You need to be able to move in the event of an attack. Those look like an unrelenting prison. And ugly too."

My shoulders shook as my giggles turned into peals of laughter, the blatant confusion on her face slipping into a slight smile as she watched me. "Hey! These are not ugly, they're fashionable. At least, they used to be. And they weren't cheap." I'd made sure to get my money's worth when Wolfe had sent me to the mall without a credit limit.

"Regardless, you need to be properly clothed if you're going to do this," she admonished me as she steered us toward the nearest bin. She sized me up, tossing me an outrageously large backpack, which we stuffed with comfortable-looking pants, shirts, sports bras, and a few sets of underwear. I was a pack-three-pairs-of-underwear-for-every-day kind of traveler, but thankfully she only gave me a slightly strange look when I asked for more.

We moved toward another bin in the back, where glints of blue and green shone out to me as the light reflected off the pieces that lay inside. I marveled at the armor that lay inside. "It's beautiful, isn't it?" She picked up a breastplate, holding it in front of her so I could see. Glittering fabric peered back at me, covering the top from wrist to throat. They didn't look super malleable, but as she picked up one sleeve, the material contorted as she moved, like a magnificent second skin. "It's made from pagu feathers, imbued with a little extra magic that helps defend the wearer. Some of the strongest armor in existence while still offering utmost flexibility. Selling one of these would catch you a mighty sum."

If she looked at me, she would probably see I had cartoon dollar signs in my eyes, but I smashed the urge down. It was not that long ago that I had been convinced to hunt down a rogue werewolf killer in exchange for ten thousand dollars, but that was barely even a thought in my mind now. My life had changed so much in such a short amount of time, in horrifying ways even, and yet I felt more passion for life than I ever had before. The realization seeped into me, rooting into my soul with an unclouded rightness.

"For you," Nia said, handing me a full set of the armor she'd now stacked into her free hand. "Treat it well, you will need it."

"Thank you," I told her sincerely, gingerly sliding them into the backpack as well, a little bit concerned at how heavy it was starting to get. She started walking towards the weapon wall and a trickle of excitement slid through me. I followed, secretly admiring the deep color of her hair as it bobbed from side to side.

"Do you dye your hair?" It was long, almost down to her butt, and I sweated just thinking about the bill it would cost to get that done.

She turned sharply to look back at me, then sighed. "I forgot you don't know all of this already. Hair color is a sign of power here. There are five royal bloodlines. Each bloodline has an affinity over a particular element, and you can always tell a royal by their hair color. Water royals have blue hair, like mine." Her regal demeanor made more sense, the way she carried herself. She walked around like a natural-born leader, confidence always at the forefront. This was a woman born to be in charge. "Fire royals have red hair, earth has brown hair, air has silver, and lightning—"

"—has blonde," I finished for her, finally understanding what the significance of my hair color was. Anyone I encountered would know I was related to Queen Tantaii, making me way easier to spot if she decided to come after us before I could get my memories back. *Shit.* "Wait, you said silver? Oliver is an air royal?"

She nodded. "Distantly, from what I understand. The air users are large in number, one of my favorite courts in the realm, actually. Aetia. The city is built in the sky, high above the treetops. Aura particularly likes to go there when we can manage to sneak away for a few days."

"I'd love to see it sometime," I told her with a genuine smile. This world was so broad, so different from my own, and the thought of exploring every inch of it made me giddy. "Does every royal family have a court?"

"Most of them," she said, sadness creasing the corners of her eyes. At the wall now, she gestured to the weapons, dozens and dozens of deadly, sharp-edged blades. "Take your pick," she urged me, not noticing my blank stare as I became overwhelmed with all the choices.

"I don't know how to use any of this," I told her, deciding honesty was the best policy when it came to weaponry. "I've only ever used a dagger I had, briefly. It was great, but I'm pretty sure it's lost to the world now." Grief at the loss frosted over my heart for a moment. The thoughtful present Callan had given me was now gone. He'd gone through all the trouble of fishing the gearshift out of the wreckage of my old car, lovingly nicknamed Stupid Bitch, and molding it into a weapon. And I'd lost it. I hoped Callan wouldn't be too mad when he found out. *Great going.*

"Well, there are plenty of daggers here." She walked me to one corner, where many daggers were indeed lining the wall, with various lengths of blades and hilts. She reached out and gripped one of my hands, startling me, and eyed it, mentally measuring the length of my forearm. She squinted at the wall, before finally reaching out to pick up a slender blade with an equally slender hilt and placed it in my hand. The weight felt good in my hand, comforting, but it didn't feel as at home against my skin as Callan's gift had. "This one will suit you. We'll have to practice with it more on the road. The more you know how to defend yourself, the better."

My ears perked up at that. "You're coming with us?"

"I wouldn't miss it for the world," she told me. A muscle in her jaw twitched as she clenched it tightly, a dark look passing over her face. "My father was one of the first to try to take a stand against Casimir after the Queen was cursed. I will soak my hands with Casimir's blood in the same way he soaked in my father's."

"I am so sorry," I told her, hoping she would feel the sincerity in my words. All roads led back to me and the choices I'd made. If I hadn't run, her father probably never would have challenged the throne and might still be alive.

"Don't ever apologize for choosing yourself." She gave my

hand a tight squeeze, my shoulders relaxing with her acceptance. "If my father had been stronger, he would be alive. It was his own naivete that got him killed. I will not make the same mistake."

Shivers ran down my spine at her words. She meant business.

"Oliver and Aura should be back soon. Nightfall is coming," she told me as we exited the armory, and true to her word, the sky was beginning to darken, both moons rising in the deepening sky. "I'll show you to your rooms for the night. Get a good night's sleep. We fly at dawn. Our journey is long."

Later, alone in the modest room I'd been given for the night, I lay on the single bed, staring at the night sky above. Most of the buildings in the stronghold didn't seem to have roofs. I would question what they did when it rained, but I bet if I asked, I'd get some throwaway answer about pagu magic. It seemed to be something they heavily relied on in their day-to-day lives.

I'd taken a quick shower in their outdoor shower before retiring to my room, grateful to see a fresh plate of more delicious fruit waiting for me. I'd been here for one day, but I already liked their way of life. If I was another person, born to a different life, maybe this could be a place I would settle. Living free, flying around during the day, trying to stick it to the man. This was my kind of place. It didn't take long for the peacefulness of the night sky to pull me under, lulling me into a gentle sleep.

I STOOD IN THE BEDROOM OF A DARK CABIN, SILENT *except for the soft chirping of the crickets wafting in from the open window. The iridescent moonlight shone in the otherwise complete darkness outside, a clear indication that this wasn't the Faerie realm. Where the fuck was I?*

A form shifted in the wooden bed before me and then froze, before a low, menacing growl sounded that made me take a few steps back, the hair on the back of my neck rising towards the heavens.

"Get out before I rip your throat out." My heart jumped as I recognized the voice. That sweltering Scottish lilt. Callan. This had to be a dream. Callan was off in the mortal realm, and I was at the Briar Stronghold, sleeping under the two-mooned sky. And yet, why was I so lucid?

"Rowan?" The complete shock and distrust in his voice put me on edge. Callan sat up in the bed, and my chest tightened at the sight of him. The blankets bunched around his hips, his toned chest on full display. He kept his eyes pinned on me, and my pulse skyrocketed as my attraction for him flared to life.

It'd only been a day since I'd seen him last, and yet it felt like it'd been forever. I'd learned so much about myself, so much about the world, and I wanted to share it with him. But this wasn't him. I'd become dependent on our partnership while we'd worked together to hunt down the killer who had been terrorizing the packs. Lexi. Callan's mate.

I took another step back, slamming the door shut on all the feelings I shouldn't have.

"This is a really weird dream I'm having," I muttered to myself as my back hit the wall, realizing the door was on the other side of the room, the imaginary panther shifter standing between me and escape. "At least in the last one, you gave me some dick. This time I'm just getting threatened." Maybe it was all the weird fruit I'd been eating?

His forehead wrinkled in surprise, casting a hooded shadow over his emerald eyes as he watched me. Slowly he slid from the bed, and a rivulet of disappointment coursed through me when I saw he was wearing a pair of loose sweatpants. This was definitely not shaping up to be a sex dream. He approached cautiously, his muscles tensed for action at a moment's notice, his eyes trailing torturously up and down my body, inspecting every inch. I looked down, flushing as I realized I was wearing exactly what I'd fallen asleep *in, a slightly too-large shirt and a pair of the simple underwear Nia had given me.*

"Where are you right now, Rowan?" He spoke low and controlled, coming to a stop a few feet away from me. He was so close I wanted to smell him, and I inhaled, frowning when I couldn't smell anything at all. He pinned me with a suspicious stare, his question more of a test than anything else.

"I'm in the Faerie realm," I replied, rolling my eyes and crossing my arms over my chest defensively. That was a mistake, my shirt riding dangerously high with the movement, and his eyes laser-focused on the newly exposed skin of my thighs before darting back up to my face. "Where is this?" If we were going to play twenty questions, I wanted to ask questions too.

"This is my house," he told me absentmindedly, a deep concern etched on his face. "I can't smell you. Why can't I smell you?"

"Don't quote me on this, but-" I leaned forward in a conspiratorial whisper, noticing the way he tensed as I got closer, "-I think this might be a dream." I knew they said if you died in a dream, you died in real life, but I liked to push the limits. If he attacked me then maybe I'd wake up from this strangeness sooner. Not that I was entirely sure I wanted that. Violent dream where I got killed? No, thanks. Spicy sex dream with the hot panther shifter? Sign me up.

"That could be true," he said, searching my eyes for any sign of deception. I held my breath at the intensity of his gaze. "Except I wasn't asleep. And this isn't a dream."

I narrowed my eyes at him. "That sounds exactly like something a dream-Callan would say."

He lifted one hand, and I stayed completely still as he reached up next to my face, going for a strand of hair. I turned my head slightly and watched as his hand went completely through, slapping the wall behind me with a thud. Now that threw me off.

"If this was fake, I'd be able to touch you," he murmured, more to himself than anything. He balled his hand into a fist, bringing it back down to his side. "I can't smell you, but I do smell...something. Magic."

"I swear I am not doing any kind of magic. My freaky talents end at lightning bolts from my hands. And maybe a portal or two, apparently." If this truly wasn't a dream, then what was this? I'd never been to Callan's house before. If this was some sort of subconscious teleportation or spell, how had it taken me to a place I'd never been before? And who was responsible?

"Come back to us."

"I can't do that. The Faerie realm needs me. There's so much you don't know." I shook my head with my denial, the truth of my statements resounding in my chest. I'd love nothing more than to go back and step back into pack life, learning to use my newfound abilities alongside my friends. But that wasn't an option for me anymore. "The realm will die without my help. I need to get my memories back."

"Then let me come with you. I can't protect you if I'm not with you." The pain in his voice was real, the only real thing I could believe tonight, but I didn't let myself be deluded into thinking that it was out of care for me. Callan was a protector, that was who he was. Former alpha of the Clover pack. Lexi murdering his entire pack had left a mark on his soul that could never be scourged. He didn't want anyone else to get hurt.

"I don't need a big scary alpha asshole to fight my battles for me," I retorted with more bravado than I possessed. I talked a big game, but I didn't have the skills to back it up and we both knew it. "Besides, shouldn't you be out there looking for your mate?" I cringed as soon as the immature words left my mouth. His mate bond was complicated, and I didn't have any right to throw it back in his face, but I stopped the apology that threatened to escape me.

Emotions flared across his face in quick succession, so fast I almost didn't catch them. Anger, then hurt, before he schooled his face into his signature indifference. I could feel his walls slamming back into place, and just like that, I was locked out again.

"You're going to be the death of me."

I opened my mouth to retort, but a sharp pain lanced through *my chest, like a knife driven straight through my heart and I doubled over, gasping for air.*

"ROWAN!" Echoes reverberated around the room as the bodiless voice shouted from every direction, the house beginning to shake. Callan looked around wildly, trying to pinpoint where it was coming from, poised to fight an enemy that he couldn't see.

"ROWAN!" The pain in my chest heightened until I couldn't breathe and it felt like I might burst. Callan grabbed for me, his hands going straight through me and knocking him off balance. My heartbeat thudded in my ears, rising until I could hear nothing else.

A sharp tug on my wrist pulled me downward, and I fell, expecting to hit the ground but I didn't. I kept falling and falling and—

My eyes shot open, the beginnings of dawn overhead, the two moons receding as the sky started to lighten. I hurtled downward, still on my back, and groaned as my body slammed back into the bed I had been sleeping in.

"Are you okay?" Oliver's worried face swam into view as the remnants of my time with Callan came flooding back to me.

"Huh?" was all I could say, my mind a jumbled mess trying to fit together all the pieces.

"I don't know if it's a good thing," Nia mused from her place in the doorway, leaning against the frame. "But things have certainly gotten more interesting since you got here."

"What the fuck was that?" A slight twinge burst to life in my lower back; I must have tweaked it when I fell back down, but the telltale itching of my accelerated healing was already kicking in. "That was the weirdest dream I've ever had. I dreamt I was visiting Callan back in the mortal realm, but it really didn't feel like a dream. More like a . . . vision or something."

Oliver looked at me with an appraising look, the gears turning behind his eyes. I waited for an explanation, but he simply shrugged his shoulders, confusion spreading across his features as he glanced towards the sky. "I didn't see any magic; I can't say for certain that I know what that was. Do you have any more hidden talents you don't know about?" he quipped, but there was a layer of mirth behind his gaze.

"Bite me," I grumbled, pushing away my disappointment at realizing it had actually been a dream. Seeing Callan again so clearly had thrown me for a loop. I could still picture him, inches from my face. *Jesus, get a grip.* I refused to let him affect me so much.

"I'll do some research and see if I can figure out what happened," Oliver assured me, exiting the hut dismissively before I could voice my protest. Call me crazy, but an edge of suspicion slithered around in my mind. Oliver did not seem the least bit concerned, and as far as I knew, floating in the air was not a part of my magical being package. I knew Fae couldn't lie, but did he know more than he was letting on?

"Get dressed, we need to get going," Nia told me before she swished back out, already clad in her armored gear, the door to my hut shutting softly behind her.

Chapter Seven

Two hours later, we stood in an outcropping toward the edge of the stronghold, readying the pagu to fly. I'd shaken off my earlier dream but stayed determined to pester Oliver about it as soon as I got the chance. The more I thought about it, the more it didn't sit right with me.

The pagu did have structured harnesses, which Aura was very vocal about hating to wear. Nia yelled at her as she tried to strap it on, the intimidating bird flapping her wings every time she tried to get close enough. "You are way too old to be acting like a child!"

'It's such an ugly color,' she scoffed, looking entirely serious. The frustrated sounds that exploded from Nia were loud as they bickered back and forth until Nia eventually managed to convince her to put on the harness. It was fairly simple, with two large side pockets for us to store gear and a little built-in seat for the rider to sit more comfortably. But Aura was right, it was ugly as fuck. Strips of white and black material were woven together in nonsensical patterns, hanging down to her sides. She looked like a chicken wearing a zebra-striped dress, and I wisely decided not to laugh.

"Pagus are vain creatures," Oliver whispered conspiratorially, making sure to keep out of earshot of Aura. "But she is particularly self-centered."

"There's no way we're all going to be able to fit on Aura," I mused.

'We won't be alone. Varus and Lithia, two of our unbonded, will be joining us,' Aura chimed in, her displeasure strong enough to cut steel. I was somewhat surprised by that. I'd just assumed that all adult pagus would have formed a bond already.

Like he was summoned, a pagu emerged from beneath the cliff where we stood, his large wingspan kicking up enough wind to cause me to take a step back or risk being knocked over. He looked a lot like Aura, with the same spiked head, razor-like beak, and shimmering feathers, but he almost doubled her in size, his eyes a darker shade of red, so dark they almost looked black. A much smaller female flew up closely behind him, her talons glinting in the sunlight as she landed surely on the ground.

'You're late, Varus,' Aura admonished, eyes pinned on the larger male. Varus's crimson eyes settled on her. Given his size, I thought he might challenge her, but he didn't, only giving her a gruff nod of acknowledgment as he tucked his wings against his frame, moving towards Nia where she held a harness ready and waiting.

'We really need to redesign these,' Varus grumbled, more to himself than anything and I snorted a laugh. His voice in my mind was low, much lower than Aura's.

'I think they make us look friendly,' the female, Lithia, said as she moved past me and over to Nia.

Once everyone was saddled, we loaded up the harnesses with our bags, readying to venture out. I had donned a similar outfit to Nia's and it was surprisingly light, molding to my body like a second skin.

"Anytime you are outside of the cloaking magic of the Briar Stronghold," Nia had told me as we had approached the takeoff zone, "you must be wearing your armor. Casimir's forces are vicious, and with Queen Tantaii back and searching for that ring, they're going to come for you. We need to get your memories back as quickly as possible. That armor could mean the difference between life and death for you." She looked me up and down grimly, and I tried not to be offended. "Especially you."

Great.

I dropped onto Varus's back, his magic immediately locking us into place as we waited for Nia to get situated, still on tentative ground with Aura after their argument earlier. Oliver made quick work of mounting Lithia's smaller form. Once we were all seated, Varus launched into the sky, climbing upwards with the strong strokes of his wings, Aura shortly following suit.

"The temple is about a week's ride from here. It won't be easy. It's nestled right in the center of the Queen's territory," Oliver called out, loud enough to be heard over the roar of the wind and wings. "We will need to take a small detour about halfway in a town called Mossemere to see an old friend who can help us travel to the Goddess's temple and hopefully get us there safely. When we are airborne, we should be relatively safe, but when we make camp . . . It will never do us harm to be over-prepared."

Without further ado set off, steadily making our way through the sky. I was grateful for the double layer of clothes I was wearing, the biting wind on my face a stark reminder of my original arrival at the Briar Stronghold. Beneath me, Varus acted as a small heater, just enough to keep the edge of chill from completely frosting me over.

"I'm Rowan!" I shouted at Varus, leaning forward so I could be as close to his ear as I could reach, making sure he heard me over the wind. He flinched underneath me, his big body jerking with the movement and I death-gripped the harness, even though the bonds around my legs never wavered.

'You don't have to yell,' his deep voice grumbled in my head as he righted his body beneath mine. *'We have very sensitive hearing. You'd have to talk in the slightest whisper for me not to hear you. And I know who you are.'*

"Everyone seems to," I muttered. I liked being invisible, able to blend into the background when I wanted to, and that wasn't something I could do anymore. Not here.

'Getting rid of that ugly yellow hair would be a good start.'

If I wasn't already held down by magic, I would have kicked the shit out of him.

"If you're going to be a dick the whole way, this is going to be a really awkward ride," I said instead, infusing as much attitude into my voice as I could. I could have said worse things, but it did not escape my notice that my survival entirely depended on this animal keeping me glued to him.

'I can do whatever I want, sweetheart. There's a reason you're on my back and not theirs.'

Ego wafted off him in droves, and I laughed. "I just assumed it was because we're both stubborn assholes," I retorted, sniffling a little in the cold front.

His chest rumbled beneath me, and it took me a few seconds to realize it was a laugh. He suddenly veered upward, flapping his wings hard as Aura and Lithia shot past us, their bewildered riders turning their heads up to see what we were doing. My breath caught in my throat as I did my best not to look behind me, which would be straight down to the unforgiving ground below us.

"What are you doing?" I screamed over the hard gushes of air generated from each stroke of his massive wings. He said nothing, continuing to ascend and I could do nothing but hold on for dear life with my arms, my legs still pinned to his sides by magic. I risked a glance below us, anger and confusion igniting in me as I saw Oliver and Nia idling on their pagus, staring up at us as we climbed further into the sky. *They weren't coming to help me.*

Finally, he stalled, coming to a pause in the air. He turned his spiked head slightly towards me, until he was able to look at me with one wine-stained eye, a mischievous glint lurking within.

'You can fly, right?' he asked me as he tumbled upside down, until the top of my head pointed straight down toward the ground.

"No, you know I can't fucking fl—" My protest was cut off

when the iron bands of magic released, my legs easily slipping out of the harness. My hands were slick with nervous sweat and my grip slipped, my body falling toward the ground far below, with nothing else to hold on to. I screamed, my arms waving wildly in the air as I tried in vain to grab onto something to break my fall. I looked for Oliver or Nia, but the world was whizzing by too fast for me to make anything out and I shut my eyes, preparing myself for death.

My ass thudded against something solid, and my eyes opened wide. Familiar solid bands guided my legs into their rightful place in the harness as my torso slammed against Varus. I looked down, where we hovered just feet above the ground below. I'd been very, very close to death.

'Control yourself. Or I will make sure you never set foot outside Briar again.' Aura's voice of rage was terrifying, every word she spoke a sharpened sword, ready for execution.

'He didn't mean any harm by it,' Lithia chimed in, her melodic voice soothing the edges of my frazzled nerves even as she defended my bully. *'He was just getting to know her.'*

"If you ever do that again, I'll kill you myself!" I'd found my voice, my body shaking with adrenaline and anger. I didn't know where one began and the other one ended. I was just a messy ball of raw nerves.

'You know I'd have never let her hit the ground,' Varus said. *'I don't make mistakes like that. I just wanted to have a little fun.'* His complete indignation at anyone thinking he couldn't handle it reminded me very similarly of another certain overconfident male I knew.

"You can have all the fun you want when this is over," Oliver demanded, staying alert as his eyes darted around us. Being this close to the ground was dangerous, made it more likely someone could stumble upon us and leave us exposed, especially if they landed eyes on me. "We have a long distance to cover before we make camp. No more messing around." Lithia launched them back in the air, and Aura soon followed after one last look toward my riding companion, a clear threat in her stare.

Varus craned his neck to look at me, and after summoning my best death glare, he shook his head slightly before launching into the air to follow the rest of our squad. As his wings beat us steadily through the air, he tilted his head back slightly. *'Do not worry, Rowan. I play rough, but we fight for the same goal. I will cut down armies for you if it means that Queen Tantaii will get what's coming for her. I will let no harm come to you.'*

It may come back to bite me later, but I believed him.

CHAPTER EIGHT

B y the time we made camp for the night, I was shivering, the incessant flying leaving me with only aches and sore muscles. The healing perks of my heritage were great, but also left me in a perpetual state of itchiness that didn't fade until I ungracefully slid from Varus's back, still irritated at him from earlier. Much of the ride had passed in silence, which was something I think we were both content with.

We'd found a small freshwater pond with a small grassy area, just enough space for two tents and a fire, which Oliver graciously used his magic to light. Food, I learned, was an abundant resource in the Fae realm. Most of the land we had travelled over was dotted with trees and forests, only the occasional village or field popping up, and fruit grew almost everywhere.

"We can just pick them off and eat them?" I asked skeptically, eyeing the spotted oranges Nia was picking from a nearby tree.

"What else would you do with them?" she scoffed, tossing me a yellow orange as she bit into one, clear juice running down her chin as she chewed. I almost lunged forward to stop her from eating the peel, but when she dove in for another bite, I figured it must be edible on this side of the realm. I hesitated, before chomping down on mine, again impressed by how delicious it was, sweetness oozing from its very center and curling into a happy ball in my tummy. Instead of a bitter, tough peel like the oranges back home, this one was more like candy, sweet and soft.

"I bet now you're going to tell me we can just drink the water, straight from the pond?" I moved toward it, intending to do just that, but the resounding, "NO!" from both Oliver and Nia stopped me. I looked between the two of them, searching for the third head they'd grown.

"You can never drink water straight from the source in Faerie," Oliver chided as he ran over, a large waterskin held in one hand. "There are a lot of medicinal herbs that grow in the bodies of water here. Drinking without purifying it first could kill you."

"How do you purify it? Boil it?"

"With magic, of course." He dipped down near the water's edge, gently letting the water flow in. He brought the full water-skin towards me, holding a hand out over the top. I watched as a golden shimmer of magic flowed into the container. He continued for a few more seconds, before dropping his hand, the magic disappearing. "Every Fae can do some semblance of magic, even if they aren't from a royal bloodline. It's not anything they can fight with, but there are some things that everyone can inherently do. Our magic counteracts the effect of anything that might be lurking in the water. The only ones immune are animals."

"I can do that?" At his nod, excitement burst through me. I ran to my backpack which was haphazardly lying next to Varus as he relaxed with Lithia and Aura, recovering from their long journey. I rummaged through it until I found the flask Nia had given to me. Varus watched me with heavy-lidded eyes, but wisely said nothing.

After I filled the flask, I looked at Oliver, almost bouncing on the balls of my feet. I was so used to knowing nothing, unable to fend for myself, and the thought of being able to actually do some successful magic had me giddy, no matter how small. "What do I do?"

"Hold your hand above the flask. Magic is all about intention.

It fits the mold you give it. Think of it like water. Without a container or guidance, it will spill everywhere if you try to move it, and you won't be able to scoop it back up. But if you can control its flow, it will go where you tell it. This will be good practice for you."

I did as he instructed, my hand held over the water, my eyes closing as I took a deep breath. "Now concentrate," he said softly. "It's not like your elemental powers, where you have to draw on it from within, like something tangible. This magic is inherent, you are born of it. It should be as easy as breathing. Just focus on your intention, and the magic will respond. It knows you."

Focus on my intention? He sounded like a religious fanatic giving a sermon. I snorted a laugh at my own thought before I could restrain it. I risked a glance at Oliver, quickly focusing back on the task when I saw his glare.

Focus on my intention. *Okaaaaaay.*

I tilted my head back slightly, letting my mind settle as I focused, the fresh air tickling the loose strands of my hair. The longer I stood, the more I could *feel* the magic that surrounded us. It was everywhere, as if every molecule of oxygen was also bonded with glittering magic. It permeated the earth beneath my feet, the sky above my head, and even in the people and animals that surrounded me. I focused inward, finding the same glittering magic woven through me, beating along with my heartbeat like a drum. I looked past the lightning that I felt, sparking but dormant, and another earthy ball of energy that must have been my shifter powers. I was definitely going to come back and explore that later.

Focus, Rowan.

I latched on to the magic inside me, urging it to go into the flask, but when I opened my eyes, nothing had moved. There was a slight shimmer in my hand, but nothing flowed into the flask the way Oliver's had. My brows furrowed, and I slammed my eyes shut, attempting again.

"Be one with the water," Oliver's irritating voice pulled my focus, and I pushed it away.

"Thanks, Mr. Miyagi." I hoped he could hear my internal eye roll. I was sick of feeling helpless and entirely useless while people came to my rescue. I needed to be able to do this. I breathed deep, pulling on the magic with as much force as I could muster.

"No, don't—" Oliver shouted, and I tried to pull back, but it was too late, as the waterskin exploded in my hand, cutting a deep gash into my palm that made me hiss. I dropped the remaining fragments of the pouch on the ground. There was definitely no coming back from that.

Nia rushed to my side, a spare cloth in her hand as she dabbed my cut gently. She looked it over before summoning a little water from the pond. It glowed brightly when it connected with my cut, and after a few seconds she pulled away, and I was good as new.

"Thank you," I told her sourly, the disappointment in myself palpable. She handed me her fully filled water skin, and I drank from it gratefully before handing it back.

"Don't thank me," she replied gently. "Faerie blood is highly powerful, and traceable. I have no doubt the Queen and her lackeys are searching for you. The less you bleed, the better." Right. Of course, she didn't do it out of the goodness of her heart.

"I didn't expect you to get it on the first try. It takes practice." Oliver slung an arm around my shoulder in a comforting gesture, but I shrugged him off. I didn't need him to coddle me. What I needed was to be able to use my magic. Determination took over, pushing my self-loathing to the side as I focused on a different prize.

My memories.

Once I had them back, I'd remember how to use my powers. And where to find this ring before Queen Tantaii found it first. I only had to make it that long.

"I'm going to turn in," I told the group, weariness tugging at my soul. Tomorrow was a new day, and that much closer to getting to our destination. I snagged another orange off a nearby tree, heading toward the tent we had set up for Nia and I to share. I hoped to be asleep before she decided to join me so I wouldn't have to make any awkward small talk.

Tomorrow I would be social, but today I would be me.

I strolled past the pagu's resting area on my way to the tent, Varus catching my eye as he regarded me. I eyed the distance between him and Lithia with interest as they lay flush against each other, almost lovingly. She had already fallen asleep, tired from the long journey, but Varus stayed awake and had watched my whole embarrassing use of magic. I glowered at him, holding on to my grudge from earlier with a steel-fisted grip, ready for a sassy remark.

'*I wasn't going to say anything,*' he voiced in my head. I narrowed my eyes at him before proceeding into the tent, settling into one of the sleeping bags we had already laid out. It was not nearly as comfortable as the ones from the mortal realm, but it would do, the itchy fabric only mildly irritating if I didn't move. I closed my eyes, waiting for the sandman to pull me under, a slight sense of anticipation running through me. Would I dream of Callan again tonight?

'*But just so you know, even children the age of five can purify water.*'

If there had been enemies near, they would have absolutely heard my aggravated scream.

CHAPTER NINE

Nia's shout woke me, and I bolted upright in the tent. The tent was already small, but it was even smaller now that there was a large oval portal swirling right in front of us. It shimmered and faltered, not at all like the steady portal Oliver had opened to get me here. This one was weak, flickering and inconsistent, but still stayed open. I peered at it, but only darkness greeted me from the other side.

"What did you do?!" Nia exclaimed as the portal held steady in the air.

"Me? I didn't do this!" She was crazy if she thought I was just out here opening portals while the drool dribbled out of my mouth.

Behind the portal, the flap to our tent opened, Oliver's shocked face barely visible from the other side. "Well, I sure as shit didn't open it," he said. The portal surged, its inky edges writhing, outlining the circular entrance hungrily. "You've only had your Fae powers unlocked for a brief amount of time. They are unpredictable, as we've already seen."

"Wait a minute." I stepped closer to the portal, squinting through the darkness. The longer I looked, the more I was able to make out shapes hidden among the shadows. I took another step closer, the edges of a bedframe coming into view, the dots connecting with my memory. "I know this place!"

I must have spoken too loudly, because the figure on the bed stirred, shooting up like a rocket when he realized what was in his bedroom. He leaped forward with a growl that sounded garbled through the wavering portal, but I recognized it all the same.

Callan.

And he was in the bedroom I had dreamt about the night before. I had never seen his house before. How had it been possible that I'd dreamt it?

"Rowan?" His confusion was blatant, and I saw him eyeing my surroundings suspiciously. "What is this?"

"Heeeeeeeeeey there . . . friend," I finished awkwardly, throwing a hand up in a pseudo wave. "Pardon the intrusion. Oliver is going to close this portal and let you get back to sleep. Aren't you, Oliver?" Extra emphasis toward Oliver, who took the hint, his hands coming up towards the portal. The golden shimmer of magic was already starting to coat his hands.

"Wait!" Callan shouted, the words almost getting lost as the portal started to shrink under Oliver's practiced guidance. Callan disappeared from view, and I squinted, barely able to make out his back as he rummaged through the drawer on his nightstand, before he ran at the portal, diving face-first through it as the opening got smaller and smaller. He crashed through, landing in a heap on top of Nia and me with a groan.

"Get off of me, you disgusting animal!" Nia lashed out toward Callan, and he groaned in pain as she sank a fist into his side.

"Ow!" he roared, but rolled off of us, somehow still graceful as he rose up to stand near Oliver.

"Are you crazy?" Oliver's gaze was serious, but a small trickle of amusement shone in his gaze as he took Callan in. His eyes darted to me briefly before they trained back on the shifter. "Do you know what can happen if a portal closes on you before you're all the way through? You can't be here, you don't belong in this realm!"

Callan stood to his full height, towering over the shorter man as his icy alpha power radiated off him in waves. Even in his sleep-wear and bedhead, my stomach did little flip-flops when I looked at him, so I glanced away, reinforcing my walls. "It was worth the risk. And I'll fucking kill you if you try to send me back."

I was sure mine weren't the only eyebrows that shot up at his words. Callan whirled around, pinning me with a stern glare. I shrank back, doing my best to wish myself invisible. "You really thought following this witch through a portal would be a good idea? Have you lost your fucking mind?" When he was mad—which he usually was when he talked to me—his Scottish lilt came to the surface, clinging to his sharp words.

"So . . . about that . . . "

AN HOUR LATER CALLAN AND I SAT AROUND THE FIRE, sipping on a fuchsia tea Nia had concocted from some of the various fruits that surrounded us in abundance. I'd finished filling Callan in on our quest, and while initially he was upset, he had now settled into begrudging acceptance. The morning air was chilly, the sun just starting to rise, and I stared off into the depths of the fire, the crackling comforting sound as the sticks and fallen logs we'd made it with burned.

I watched Callan, for what exactly I wasn't sure. He'd taken the information in stride, attention pinned on the fire as I'd shared what I had learned. His usual stoic face was in place, a hard mask that prevented me from gauging his reaction as he listened. Would he still accept me, knowing that I was half-Fae? Would the rest of the pack? There'd been no time to discuss or digest the information before I'd run through the portal. They could hate me for all I knew; it'd been my fault that Evie had died in the first place. Lily could never forgive me for that. I'd brushed the few tears that trickled from my eyes as I recounted my events of being kidnapped by Ruby, held in the in-between, and tortured.

By Lexi.

"Is everyone back at the pack okay?" I asked Callan softly.

He nodded, his midnight hair bouncing slightly with the movement. "They're fine. Just extremely worried, after you left us there like that," he replied, sourness edging his tone.

"I'm sorry," I told him, and I meant it. I'd give anything to hop back into a portal to the mortal realm, to go live in the forest and learn how to use my powers, and to forget all about my fucked-up heritage. Yeah, I meant it. "But now you understand what's at stake. I don't feel like I really had a choice."

"There is always a choice." His knee bumped mine from where we sat around the fire, a harmless gesture that left a lingering heat where it touched me. "And yours was shitty. Lily is a frantic mess."

"But she's alive. I need to get my memories back so I can make sure she stays that way. All of you."

"I know. And then we'll go back." Our eyes locked in understanding, and I breathed a sigh of relief. There was no judgement in his gaze, no hatred like I had expected.

"Why did you jump through the portal?" Our eyes met, and I stilled at the emotions swirling in their depths. He said nothing, the silence stretching a little too long. He broke eye contact as he stood, reaching into his pocket and sliding a familiar slender object from his baggy sweatpants. "I went back for this; I figured you might need it."

I gasped in delight, snatching the dagger from him, the hilt fitting in my hand like a glove.

"I thought I lost it!" I exclaimed before I could hold my tongue, gripping the blade happily to my chest. It was stupid to be so attached to an inanimate object, but Callan had made the dagger for me from the remnants of my favorite car. Having it was like having a piece of her with me, and it immediately brought comfort and calm to my soul. Holding it in my hand felt *right*.

"You dropped it when Roxy kidnapped you." A smirk played at the corner of his mouth as he watched my excitement, but I was too happy to be worried about being judged. "I shouldn't have let her get the jump on us like that." He stared into the flames, a tortured look passing across his face.

Flashbacks of that night with Lexi flitted through my mind, anger bristling in my chest.

"How is it that your mate is still alive?" I pinned him with a hard stare. I couldn't ignore the voice in the back of my head that called out how suspicious that all was. His mate murders an entire pack, and he supposedly carried out the justice, but now she's working with my evil family to destroy the realms. Something didn't add up.

"I have no fucking idea," Callan responded after a pause, raising his eyes to meet mine. "I gave her that scar on her face. Right before I ripped out her throat." His harsh tone gave me pause, and I could almost taste the hatred wafting off him. He held steadfast, confident in his conviction that he had killed Lexi. Yet she was alive, and her throat was most definitely intact.

"Do you feel her? Can't mates read each other's minds or something?" I had no idea, but after all these surprises, I almost expected it to be a thing.

He snorted. "I haven't been able to feel her since the night I killed her. Or thought I did. I held her in my arms, Rowan. I watched the blood pour out of her. I dug the grave I buried her in. There is no way she should be alive."

"Guess that explains why you didn't die." At his confused look, I continued, "Lily told me when one mate dies, the other one usually does to."

"When I killed her, I expected to die. I waited to die. But it never came. I guess now I know why," he added, a bitter bark of laughter escaping him.

"You still have a bond," I said, keeping my voice level and even when I felt anything but. "Fae can see magic, and I saw it back there. It was weak, and damaged in some places, but still intact."

"It doesn't matter," he said sharply. "She did incredibly heinous things, of her own volition. My bond with her was broken the day she killed my pack. I have no mate."

"Maybe she was magicked," Nia offered, the cogs in her head turning behind her wise face as she stepped up to the fire with us. "Or you were."

"You think I wouldn't have noticed?" he snarled in reply, the mere thought of having been spelled setting him on edge. She glowered back, her hackles raised as she went on the defensive.

"Relax, panther. It was just a suggestion." I looked between the two of them, wondering if I was going to have to break up a fight eventually. Nia hadn't fought in front of me, but I had no doubt getting caught in between them would result in my gruesome death.

Oliver joined us, holding a hand above the fire, and we watched in awe as the flames floated off of the burning pile of wood and absorbed into Oliver's outstretched hand. Seeing my face, he winked at me, a small smile turning up the corner of my mouth. He turned to Callan, quirking a brow. "We need to get back on the road soon. Are you sure you're up for the task? The goddess's temple is in the heart of enemy territory. The likelihood we get spotted and killed is higher than not."

A feral smile twisted his handsome features as Callan stood to mirror Oliver. "If she goes, I go."

CHAPTER TEN

Much to my chagrin, it was decided that Callan would ride on Varus's back with me, given he was the largest of the three pagu. My protests fell on deaf ears as Callan crowded behind me, forcing me to sit as far forward as I could.

"I'm sure Oliver would love to ride with you," I hinted at Callan as he settled into place behind me on Varus. The harness was barely big enough for two, which meant Callan had to get very close to me to be able to also hang on, his chest flush against my back. The magic iron bars held our legs in place as usual, but my every nerve stood at attention to the sweltering panther shifter glued to my back.

"I don't want to ride with Oliver." His hot breath tickled my ear as he spoke, and a slight shiver ran through me. I could feel his heartbeat where it thudded against me, strong and steady.

'Have the hots for the panther shifter, do you?' Varus's amused voice sounded in my head, and I held back the spicy retort I had loaded. Judging by Callan's lack of reaction, he'd only said that in my head. I refused to think about my body's reaction to Callan, because then I'd have to ask myself why I cared. One night with

the guy going down on me and it was like I'd turned into a smitten schoolgirl.

We flew for most of the day, only coming down for small breaks before getting back in the air. I had a new appreciation for the pagu and their incredible stamina, even if Varus was a dick. Slowly I adapted to having Callan behind me, who was not really one for small talk, but I managed to get some grunts and nods out of him occasionally. Even though I was forced to share my space, I found it comforting, his body heat radiating around me and easing the chill that usually settled in me while we rode. But I would die before I ever told him that.

When we finally made camp, we were all so tired from our rough morning, a quick dinner was all we could manage before retreating to our tents.

"Where is the meat?" Callan grumbled as he looked down at the offered orange I held outstretched in my hand. A giggle bubbled in my chest, but I fought it down, feigning a look of sympathy.

"There is no meat."

"How can there be no meat?"

"Fae only eat fruit."

"How can someone survive off only fruit? What the hell am I supposed to eat?" The look of disbelief on his face broke me, and I burst out laughing at the pure despair coming from him.

"You're not going to die. Fruit is good for you." Driving my point home, I bit into the fruit, closing my eyes as the familiar sweetness burst over my tongue. My tastebuds danced happily inside my mouth. I narrowed a look at him. "Is the big bad shifter afraid of a little fruit?" It was probably unwise to tease him, but I couldn't help it. He was a panther shifter, but right now he just seemed like an angry housecat.

The orange was snatched from my hand and he bit into it aggressively, his eyes never leaving mine as he chewed. I'd never considered a man eating fruit to be sexy before, but there was a first time for everything.

"I love that attitude of yours," he told me.

"Really?"

"No."

Bang!

The earth shook with the force of the explosion. I jolted awake, Nia already rolling into a standing position, producing a thin sword in her hand within seconds. She spared a glance at my awkward form as I pulled myself up, picking up my dagger from where I'd left it next to my sleeping bag, the weight comforting in my grasp. I was already wearing my armor, thanks to Nia's urging that we sleep in protective wear while in hostile territory.

"We are under attack," she said seriously, head tilted as she listened intently.

"I hadn't noticed." I resisted the urge to roll my eyes, but just barely, holding my knife out defensively in front of me.

Bang!

Nia grabbed my free hand, hauling me along behind her as she pulled us out of the tent and into the pure chaos outside. I coughed, the air thick with smoke that clouded my vision, threatening to suffocate me. A large, hulking shadow darted past us, and I let out a little gasp as I stepped to the side. Deep growls could be heard to our left, but I couldn't make out anything through the dense smoke. A pained shout cut through the haze like a shot through my chest.

Callan.

Nia's grip tightened on me, pulling me flush against her side. "Shadow beasts," she said grimly, her eyes scanning for enemies. "We need to get out of here. Conjured from the depths of ash under the fire royal's palace, they leave nothing but death and destruction in their wake."

"Fabulous," I breathed, trying not to make too much noise

and get discovered. Shadow beasts sounded ominous as fuck, and I really didn't want to learn why they went by that name.

'*NIA!*' Aura's shout was one we both could hear, and Nia swore before gripping me tighter and running off, deeper into the smoke. She ran like she was on a mission, and I realized she must be able to pinpoint where Aura is through their bond.

After a few seconds Aura swam into view, surrounded on three sides by these shadow beasts. I blinked a few times as my eyes skirted over them. They wavered where they stood, as if I couldn't quite focus on their form while looking directly at them. They were made of smoke, large and hulking, greatly resembling a wolf pack. Sharp, glinting teeth hung menacingly from their mouths as they surrounded their prey. Aura was bleeding, one of her wings torn and oozing, but still she fought, her talons whipping toward them. The shadows disappeared for a moment when she sliced through them, but within seconds they reformed and were back on the attack. Aura was tiring, her movements slowing as her breathing became more labored.

"Target the eyes," Nia told me as she readied her sword, her free hand already summoning the water from the pond. "It's their weakest point, their power center. Take out both eyes and they'll stay dead. And don't use your lightning powers, they'll only absorb it." *Stay dead?* With that, she launched forward, sword slicing and water whipping like an avenging angel as she tried to help Aura.

The shadow nearest to me backed up at Nia's explosive entrance, pivoting to turn to me with a snarl. I bent my knees slightly, leaning forward with my dagger death-gripped in my hand.

I was not going to die here.

With no warning he launched at me, a much higher leap than I was expecting. I stabbed my knife out just when he was about to land, a strange sensation enveloping my hand as it just went through his body. He solidified, knocking me onto my back, going straight for my throat.

I brought my arm up just in time, my knife piercing through his chin, the blade peeking at me from between his open jaw and he went limp above me.

Did I kill him?

My breath panted as I looked in his face, mere inches away from mine. Nia said to destroy the eyes, but he seemed pretty freaking dead to me. I shrugged him off my dagger, pleasantly surprised when the blade pulled away clean. I look around for Nia, who was busy dispatching the last shadow beast, her blade slicing through one eye as an ice blade she had formed in the other stabbed straight through his remaining eye. With only one foe to face, Aura had already killed her opponent, his body lying in a limp heap in front of her.

I looked around the clearing, but it was still permeated with smoke, and I drew in closer to my companions as I searched frantically. Where were Callan, Oliver, and the other pagus?

Bang!

There! An explosion to our left, deeper into the surrounding trees as a bright explosion of fire flickered beyond the smoke. "We have to go help them!" I shouted to Nia as I started off in that direction, not bothering to look back at them as I raced to help my friends.

"Rowan, watch out!" Nia shouted as she started running toward me, but it was too late. I was knocked face-first into the dirt, my knife skidding out of my hand, grateful for my armor as he tried to slash through it but couldn't. I screamed when his teeth bit into the skin of my exposed neck, taking a chunk with him as he ripped away. A loud roar ripped through the night, an ebony panther darting over me, flinging the shadow beast backward off me with a sickening crunch as he hit the ground. A small grunt of effort came from Nia as she finished the animal off, her sword lancing through his eye.

"I told you through the eyes. Always through the eyes," she huffed as she withdrew her blade from his face, ever present and alert as she scanned for more enemies.

Callan's panther nudged my face as I rolled over, giving me a gentle lick of his scratchy tongue which I pushed away. "I'm fine."

He dipped his head, setting a heavy paw on my leg as I sat up so he could talk in my mind. *'Oliver needs our help.'*

"Where are Varus and Lithia?" I questioned as I pushed myself up, reclaiming my blade and following Callan through the trees, Nia and an injured Aura trailing behind us.

'They snuck up on us while we were asleep, and Lithia got injured. I lost sight of them in the scuffle, until I saw them. Flying away.' Rage quivered in Aura's voice, mixed with pain and a loathing I didn't understand. *'I told you they shouldn't be on this mission.'* Her anger turned toward Nia, who recoiled slightly under the brunt of Aura's disapproval.

Another loud bang broke us into a run, Nia's judgement was something to be questioned later once we found Oliver. We halted as we ran through a gap in the trees, sweat immediately sticking to my back as we came upon Oliver and the source of the loud explosions became immediately apparent.

A loud cackle came from the halfling as he danced within his protection, surrounded on all sides by at least a dozen shadow beasts. They snarled but didn't approach the flames, cautiously skirting around him. A raging fireball was being weaved in his hands, and when it was finally big enough, he launched it through the flames, attacking his target like a heat-seeking missile as it tried to turn and run. The second the flames connected, a loud bang sounded, the shadow creature exploding upon impact, disintegrating into dust. He immediately went back to building up the next one, hands weaving as sweat dripped down his brow.

"Risen by the ashes, destroyed by the flame," Nia commented as she eyed the situation keenly, calculating the best way to approach this new information. The shadows hadn't noticed us yet, and Oliver was making fast work of his giant fireball. "Aura and I will take the right, you guys take the left. That should cause enough of a distraction that Oliver can take out the rest." She turned to go, before quickly pivoting back to look at me. "And what are you going to do, Rowan?"

"Stab them in the fucking eye," I ground out, my neck itching where the edges of the bite started to heal. It didn't make it hurt any less, and I was rabid to enact my revenge on its spawn mates. Satan siblings.

Whatever.

'Stay behind me,' Callan said as he brushed against me, prowling towards the nearest beast. He was a vicious shadow as he pounced on the nearest one, diving straight for its eyes and quickly dismantling it before moving on to the next. I stayed close, my dagger held out in front of me defensively. A burst of fire from the right drew my attention for a brief second, a giant flame bursting from Aura's mouth and incinerating one of the shadows.

Holy. Shit.

Two more shadows turned towards me and I lasered in on them as they advanced with a predatory stillness, widening into a half circle, boxing me in. Weighing my options, I lunged toward the one on my left, figuring the element of surprise would be my only chance. I hissed as a claw embedded itself into my hip, just managing to slip in between the pieces of my armor. I plunged my dagger into one eye, grimacing as I gripped and twisted, pulling away with a wet squelch. The beast weakened, and I pulled the knife back, grimly sinking it into the next eye.

A loud growl behind me caused me to pivot, yanking the dagger out as fast as I could as I turned, the beast crumpling limply to the ground as I stared into the face of the next. Callan, sleek and powerful in his feline form, tore into my opponent before I could react, rendering him dead within seconds. As our last enemy fell, so did Oliver's, the final shadow beast igniting with a blast, the wall of fire dissipating. The only evidence of its existence was the scorched earth where it had stood.

We looked around at each other. Much to my embarrassment, Callan was now back into his human form, entirely naked. I kept my eyes firmly trained on his face, not noticing one bit the way his toned muscles shifted as he moved, the dirt and grime of the forest battle only serving to make him look even more formidable.

"Let's get out of here," Oliver commanded as Nia tended to Aura's injury. "Where are Varus and Lithia?"

'I do not know, and frankly, I don't care.' The fire in her words still burned, a pained look in her eyes as Nia's water shone over her wound, working her magic. The pain quickly faded into relief, and I could see the drooping wing start to knit back together. *'They are a bonded pair. I don't know why you thought it wise to bring two mated pagu on a mission, child. Especially that one.'*

Varus, it had to be.

"I expected more from them," Nia said sharply. Even though her words were firm, her healing hands never wavered. "Everyone deserves a second chance. I guess I was wrong." She spit the words out like she was being forced, and I knew it took a lot for her to say it.

"I don't understand," I looked at Oliver and Callan, who both wore equal expressions of confusion that helped me feel a little less alone.

'They used to have riders, at one point. Before they were mated. Their bonded ended up in a relationship together, and as they spent more time together, so did Varus and Lithia. They decided to mate, but on a raid gone wrong, both of their Marked were lost.' Aura said forlornly, lost in her memories.

"That's really sad." The bond Nia had with her Aura seemed filled with love, even when they sometimes went at each other's throats. At the end of the day, the others were still their first priority. That was obvious to me after watching them fight together. "I thought you said pagu have a soul bond with their bonded?"

'Normally they do. But Varus and Lithia formed a stronger bond, even stronger than the ones they had with their bonded. It's never happened before. Given the choice, they chose each other over their Marked, and both of their riders perished while they saved each other.'

84

"We cannot stay here any longer," Callan interrupted into the silence, snapping us out of our heads.

"We'll have to go on foot from here," Nia observed as she looked around at the remnants of our camp. Most of our supplies had remained intact, given the shadow beasts weren't looking for loot and more looking to rip out our throats with their teeth. Nia kicked the dirt angrily, crossing her arms over her chest.

"Aura can't carry all four of us, and her wing will need at least a day before she can support flying long distances again while the muscles continue healing."

Oliver nodded, already picking up and storing gear in preparation to leave. "Then we walk. We are not that far from Mossemere. We can be there by nightfall if we hurry, and I must insist that we do."

Chapter Eleven

Mossemere was a certifiable shithole.

That was mean, but the state of the town was abysmal, and I was shocked to see such harsh conditions in a world that had so far only shown me its beauty and splendor. If you didn't count the vaporous assholes that had tried to kill us.

"You can't come with us, Aura," Nia told her with a forlorn look. Pagu were a rare breed, and we didn't need any extra attention drawn on ourselves than necessary. "Find a place to stay the night, just stay in range. We will find a place to sleep in town and reconnect tomorrow. And you, put this on." She threw a large cloak my way, and after a second of confusion I realized why. *My hair.* I begrudgingly put it on, sliding the hood over my head. The sky was overcast in the dimming light, the weather not too different from how it was in the mortal realm.

After a brief silent goodbye, Aura took off into the sky, but I had no doubt she'd stay within range to still connect with us if needed.

After a calculating look over our ragtag group, Oliver took the lead as we walked into the decrepit town. Downtrodden buildings lined the streets in various states of disrepair—broken stones and drafty ceilings everywhere. Dozens of people milled about even though the sun was setting and life should've been winding down.

Apprehensive eyes darted out at us as we passed, a mixture of curious yet fearful, most of their hair in shades of various blacks or grays. Scanning the crowd, I realized no one had one of the royal hair colors, and many of the eyes glanced over Nia's blue hair with reverence. The hood around my golden mane tightened as I gripped it as close to my body as possible to stay hidden. I stepped closer to the group, nervous, accidentally bumping into Callan as I did. I clumsily skipped forward to regain my space, but strong hands gripped me from behind, managing to both steady me and rock my nerves simultaneously as the heat of Callan's hands permeated my clothes.

"Sorry," I mumbled, not quite ready to push out of his grasp but doing it anyway.

"Don't be," his husky voice replied. He stepped around me, crowding into me and I backed up, irritation sparking at me as I came level with Nia. *What was he doing?* I looked up, coming face to face with the back of the ill-fitting armor he wore, which he'd been forced into by Oliver, who'd threatened to send him back if he didn't cooperate. Then it clicked.

He was protecting me.

From any potential harm, but also from prying eyes. With the guys in front, I had a lot more of a shield as we walked through the town. Normally I would have kicked and screamed about being treated like I was helpless, but in this moment, I was grateful for it. And maybe even a little bit touched that he had noticed. But I would take that to my grave.

"Do all the towns look like this?" I whispered to Nia, not wanting to be overheard by anyone that might be within earshot.

"A lot of them do, yes," she replied, staying on alert as we walked, even as she talked with me. "Casimir doesn't take our magic, but he certainly likes to take everything else. He visits towns and forcibly enlists for his army, and then enacts ridiculous quotas for the towns to fill until there's nothing left for them besides food. He particularly likes to take the teenagers. But if the town fights back, he kills the ones he took. A lot of these towns had to learn the hard way."

My chest tightened as I tried to imagine myself in their shoes. What a horrible way to live, under a horrible person like that, constantly in fear. No wonder they looked the way they did. The more I learned about my so-called family, the more the black pit of hatred in my stomach grew, an empty hole of negativity and resentment. I hated everything they stood for. And I was going to put a stop to it.

We approached what looked to be a rundown tavern, its front door barely hanging on its hinges and yet packed with people. Despite their circumstances, raucous laughter poured from the dimly lit interior.

"In here?" This didn't look like the place to be having a clandestine meeting to discuss how to sneak us into the Queen's inner kingdom to get my memories back. Maybe to plan how to rob a grocery store, but not this.

"Have patience," Oliver said irritably, pushing his way into the bar as we followed suit. It was just as dingy on the inside as it was on the outside, but the throng of people did well to disguise our entrance, no one even glancing our way. "Looks just like it did last time I was here. I'm impressed."

There were a lot of words I'd use to describe the bar, but impressive was not one of them.

He pushed through the bodies, heading toward a door in the back of the bar, behind the counter. "Stay close, it's just over here." He nodded to the bartender who watched us with a close eye, and then we pushed through, the noise of the bar immediately fading as we moved, the door slamming shut behind us. I thought it would be another room, but it turned out to be stairs, and we descended, continuing until my calves burned and I was slightly out of breath. I bumped into Callan's back in front of me as he came to an abrupt stop, Nia doing similarly behind me, and we stumbled.

"Stop moving!" Oliver shouted, as if we had a choice, but Callan steadied, the rest of us following suit.

"What is that?" Callan asked, staring at something I couldn't see from where I was behind him in the narrow stairwell.

"Do you trust me?" Oliver asked, a glint of excitement in his voice that made me nervous.

"Maybe?" I said after no one spoke. He'd done nothing to give me pause so far, but you could never be too careful.

"Well, if you want to get your memories, then you're going to have to jump!" His last words faded out as he jumped, his voice echoing slightly around the chamber. I peered past Callan, eyes widening into saucers as I looked at what was in front of us. The stairs had stopped, but not only that, the entire building had stopped. We stood on the precipice of a cliff. Straight ahead and above was open air, but below was a glimmering blanket of clouds, like a heaven-sent forbidden bed.

"I'll go first. Don't come down until I tell you it's okay." Callan didn't wait for the sassy response I'm sure he knew I was preparing. I'd let him protect me a little, but bossing me around was an entirely different story. He gave me a stern look before jumping into the clouds below, and I lurched forward with a gasp. I listened hard for a few moments, but Callan never called out.

Fuck.

"Do or die," Nia said as she slipped past me. She looked down, giving her hips a little shake before she leaped off with a dive that would have made an Olympian proud.

I stepped up to the edge, a cool breeze wafting through my hair and tickling my neck. There was no evidence my companions had even jumped down, the unmarred clouds staring back up at me. *Don't be a bitch. You're not going to die here.*

I took a few steps back, shaking out the nerves in my hands as I gathered my courage. I wasn't usually bad with heights, but jumping off a cliff with no safety net seemed counterintuitive to my survival. Closing my eyes, I took a deep breath, giving myself a running start as I leapt with both feet off the stone to what I hoped wasn't my sudden and preventable death.

Going through clouds was about what I thought walking through a horny ghost would be like: cold and slightly wet. I plummeted, my eyes struggling to see as I whipped downward, tears streaming from the corners of my eyes as I fell, until I just gave up and shut them, accepting my fate. Just when I thought I would go splat, my body seized, as if an invisible force had grabbed me, stopping my momentum. I opened my eyes, looking around with shock.

"I told you she wouldn't scream," a tall, handsome Fae said to Oliver, who stood next to him as they all watched me. I hung upside down, but even then, I could see his silver hair, identical to Oliver's, with artfully coifed curls adorning his head. This was a man who owned a mirror and actually used it.

He waved a hand lazily, and my body flipped upright, my feet gently landing on the ground as I caught my balance. Callan stepped beside me, half-shielding me with his body like the over-protective oaf that he was, but I sidestepped him, wanting to stand on my own two feet.

"Hi, Ollie," the man said, a charming smile splitting across his face. Confused, I looked at Oliver, thinking he was talking to him, but both of their eyes were trained on me as the puzzle pieces fell into place. Ollie was a nickname for Olette, not Oliver.

He knew me before.

The sparkle in his eyes dimmed a little as he watched for my reaction. "When Oliver told me you'd erased your memories, I can't say I believed it, but I guess it must be true. What a shame, we used to have a lot of fun together. Before we trapped your mother in the ground and you left me." He gave me a conspiratorial wink, and Callan shifted uncomfortably beside me. Neither of us liked the familiarity in which he spoke. But there was a layer of hurt to his voice, still fresh and raw even after five hundred years. It made sense that I hadn't cursed the Queen alone, but why would I have just left him, when I had brought Oliver with me?

"I go by Rowan now," I told him sternly. Without my memories, Olette didn't exist. She felt like an outsider, like a case of mistaken identity. I had no idea who she had been, only who I was now. And I didn't know that we were still the same person, not anymore, after all this time. How could we be?

"Who are you?" I was straight and to the point. I didn't love the way he'd insinuated we had a history, toying with the information like he had something over me when he knew my memories were gone. What was with everyone and not just giving answers straight up?

"Finn." He raised a hand in greeting, and it was then that I noticed he only had one arm, his right arm cut off just below the cusp of his shoulder. He wore simple armored leathers, the garments modified so only his intact arm was sleeved. "Finneas Aelous Rosewing, but if you call me Finneas, I will cut you." That charming smile flashed again, his pearly whites on full display, but there was a level of danger and power behind them that told me he would make good on his threat.

"And what are we to each other, Finneas?"

He smirked, taking a few steps forward toward me, but halted in his tracks as Callan stepped forward with a menacing growl. Finn was tall, but Callan still had him beat, both in height and raw, dangerous energy, and he was wise to stop where he was as he eyed the panther shifter warily.

"Well, *Ollie*," he started, matching my energy, "I believe the term you so lovingly liked to hate was betrothed?"

Chapter Twelve

"**W**hat?!" Callan's voice melded with mine as we simultaneously exclaimed our outrage. Finn tilted his head back, a deep laugh escaping him as he looked between us.

"Don't worry, darling. It was arranged." He stepped closer to us, steadfastly ignoring the angry, overbearing shifter next to me as he approached. "That's very common in Fae relationships. Not to say there wasn't a time where I hoped we might work out, but I can't say that you shared the same sentiment."

"Why is it so common?"

It was Nia who gave me clarity. "No one has found their true mate in centuries, so we have arranged marriages to ensure our race continues, and our politics."

I regarded Finn. He was good-looking, sure, but I didn't feel attracted to him in the slightest. I would think if the Olette version of myself had a hard-on for him, I would feel some type of way too. Besides, I liked my men with a little more grit, a nice sharp edge of nothing to lose. My eyes strayed to Callan, and I quickly focused back on Finn. *Stop it.* "What is a true mate?"

"I've heard it's similar to the way your shifters have mates in the mortal realm. But true mates transcend everything. Time, realms, races. As long as one half of the mated couple is Fae. They used to be common back when the portals remained open—that's how most halflings came about—but no one has seen a pair since they closed."

"How do you know when you have a true mate?" I avoided eye contact with absolutely everyone, especially the surly man next to me, who not that long ago had his face buried between my thighs as he ate me out all night under the Mating Moon. I was definitely not going to look at him.

Finn gave me a knowing smile, his cerulean eyes glinting in the dim lighting of the cavern we stood in. "Fae are a spiritual people, deeply ingrained in the magic of our traditions that flow through our reality. It's different for every couple. I personally have never met one. The legends are all different. Sometimes it's an instant bond, sometimes a dream, sometimes a friendship that blossomed into a true bond. No one really knows, but the running theme in all the stories is one thing—you'll know it when you know it. True mates are bonded from the very depths of their souls, in mind and body."

Of course. Cryptic like everything else in my life. I don't know why I was so disappointed by his answer. Okay, yes, maybe I had a . . . thing for Callan. Not even a thing. Just a very small, miniscule, super-duper tiny, unimportant crush. And probably only because of the feel of the touch of his tongue on my—never mind. Either way, he already had a mate, so there was no way he could be mine, true mates or not. There was someone out there for me, maybe, but it wasn't Callan.

When I first got to the pack and learned about mates, I'd thought it was the most outrageous idea I'd ever heard. Immediately bonding with someone who you didn't even know and being told you were just supposed to be in love now? But that was before I saw the way they lived, living life on the edge with open hearts, full of life and love. It made being part of something like that seem a lot more bearable.

It's easy to judge when you're always on the outside.

I swallowed hard, pushing all heated thoughts out of my head as I forced myself back to the conversation. Luckily, Oliver seemed over the true mates talk, and I briefly wondered if he'd ever found his own before the portals closed. He had silver hair, which made him an air royal just like Finn. If he and I had been politically matched up, maybe Oliver had too.

"Thank you for heeding my call and sheltering us," Oliver said, effectively changing the subject as he got back to our task at hand. "We need your help. The Queen sent a pack of shadow beasts after us last night. Two of our pagu abandoned the mission, which leaves us on foot from here. Getting to the Primoris Temple unnoticed was already going to be a challenge by flight, but getting through the city on foot . . ." He didn't say it, but he didn't have to. We wouldn't make it through.

"The second you told me . . . Rowan was with you, I would have done anything you asked," he said, a gentleness in his eyes as he looked at me. I didn't know how I felt about him yet, but I appreciated his willingness to use my name. "We never got married, but man, were you my best friend. Right up until the very end. I'd like my friend back." He shook his memories off, turning to Oliver determinedly. "I know these tunnels like the back of my hand. I will get you to where you need to go. You can rest with the refugees tonight, and then we'll set off first thing in the morning."

"Refugees?" Nia asked. It was the first time she'd even seemed interested in the conversation we'd been having. Something told me she could not care less about mates, not when she had the fate of a whole society resting on her shoulders as their commander. I didn't think I could ever carry that kind of responsibility.

He gestured toward a branch of the tunnel, motioning for the group to follow him through the narrow passageway. As we walked, he said, "Since Casimir took over, the realm has been in disarray. There are very few towns still able to withstand his rule. I challenged him the night you left, Rowan, but I lost. He kept my arm, but I'm lucky I escaped with my life after what we did to the

Queen. He nodded toward Nia, whose lips tightened into a grim line. I heard your dad wasn't so lucky. My condolences. Niko was a good man."

"Thank you," she said politely, eyes trained straight ahead.

"When I lost the challenge, my family disowned me." His face was weary, the hurt from that banishment still striking a chord in him even after all these years. "After wandering from town to town and not being able to help anyone, I decided to do something about it. Some people run, instead of subjecting their children to the weight of his cruelty. We created hidden towns on the outskirts of the realm that we're able to funnel people to. But it's very secretive, and we run it through underground tunnels a group of earth royals helped me make. Took at least seventy-five years."

"You *made* them?" I asked incredulously, thoroughly impressed. This guy had wanted to help so much, he'd blasted tunnels underground for longer than most mortals were even alive.

He beamed at me as we rounded another branch that opened up into a much larger room, this one furnished with everything someone would need to spend the night. The tall, arching ceiling of the cave gave the room the semblance of space, and few people milled about. There were three additional branches to this one, each with a sign leading towards a different name of a town. Nia looked out around the room in awe. "This is incredible. We had no idea you were running this type of operation."

"Then that means we're doing something right," he rocked back on his heels, pride blooming on his face. He turned to the group, his expression serious. "I can get you right to the temple. You'd only have to cover maybe two miles once you exit the tunnel to get there, but once you're inside, no one can touch you. Not even Casimir can break into the Prim Temple, guarded by ancestral magic. Not until you exit."

"That sounds easy enough," I blurted. It sounded like

nothing more than a long hike and I'd be free to get my memories back.

"By now she has to know where we're headed," Nia mused, a grim expression on her face. Her battle-trained mind was already working out all the ways this could go sideways.

"Then we fight our way through." Fierce determination was etched into Callan's face, into the rigid set of his body. It warmed my heart to know he cared enough to go on this journey with me when he could have just as easily not. This was my fight; it didn't have to be anyone else's. "You can't get us any closer?"

"I will get you as close as I possibly can, but I can only take you so far. There's a high likelihood we're intercepted, and I need to ensure my tunnel systems are not discovered. I'm helping you, but my first priority will always be to my people."

He walked us over to a corner of the room where a few makeshift tents stood, seemingly unoccupied. "You guys look terrible. Rest up for the night, truly rest, and I'll be back in the morning." He stared at us as we all looked around warily, none of us willing to relax. "You're safe here. That cloud you passed through? I created it using an enchanted object. It will sear the skin from the bones of anyone who dares enter with ill intent."

"An enchanted object?" Nia asked sharply. She'd said what we were all thinking. *Could it be the ring?*

"It's not the ring, if that's what you're getting at. Rowan took that with her when she left." His tone was more accusatory than I was comfortable with, but he had a point. I was the idiot who had taken it and then forgotten where I'd put it. "I've made it a sort of passion of mine, tracking down enchanted artifacts, but I've never been able to locate that one."

"Will you tell me the story of what happened? Maybe it would help me jog my memories." Having Finn with us was a silver lining I hadn't expected. He was there when I'd cursed the Queen, and if we'd really been best friends, he'd be able to fill me in on a lot of my former life's blanks. I'd take advantage of the days we had to travel and pick his brain as much as possible.

He nodded, before he turned and walked back toward the entrance of the cave. I didn't know where he lived, but it didn't seem like he slept down here with the other refugees. "I can't wait," he called over his shoulder as he went.

"Is Aura going to be alright?" I asked Nia as we got settled around the sparse campsite.

"She'll be fine," the blue-haired girl replied as she peeked inside the tent, nodding with satisfaction that it was up to her standards. "I sent her home."

"You what?"

"She wouldn't be able to follow us down here, and I'd worry leaving her alone so long if she was to trail us from the sky, above enemy territory. It is better that she return home and check on things, and on her way back she will see if she can find Varus and Lithia."

"What will happen to them?" It was incredibly shitty that they would leave us in the middle of battle like that, when our lives were on the line, but since they were a bonded pair and Lithia was injured . . . I didn't really blame Varus for making that choice. I'd probably make the same one myself. I only hoped that they were okay, but I kept my opinions to myself.

"That depends on Aura," she said firmly, doubt clouding her gaze. "I leave the pagu politics to her."

A tall, dark-haired figure caught my eye by a firepit set up near the tent, casting shadows across the cave walls. Excusing myself with Nia, I sidled up next to him, wrapping my arms around my body in a comforting gesture in the slight draft of the cave. I looked up at Callan beneath my lashes, not knowing what I wanted to say but knowing I needed to say something. He glanced at me, and he didn't seem to know either, so we stood there, warming our hands by the fire in comfortable silence. With someone else the quiet might have bothered me, but with Callan, it was peaceful. No expectations, and no pressure. It just was.

A few minutes passed, and then he turned, setting off toward the tents. He stopped, turning to look back at me.

"Betrothed, huh?" He wore his tell-tale stone face, not willing to give an inch away of what he could be feeling beneath the surface. His eyes were dark with something I couldn't name, and I narrowed a look at him, my calmness replaced by a rabid irritation he always seemed to bring out of me.

"How's your mate?" I challenged. It was a low blow, but if he wanted to play stupid games, he would win stupid prizes. His question was simple and shouldn't have enraged me as much as it did. I didn't have a betrothed, or fiancé, or whatever you wanted to call it. And even if I did, he had no right to ask me about him when he had his own mate out running in the world.

His emerald eyes glared back at me, and without another word he turned on his heel, disappearing into his tent as I glared at his back.

CHAPTER THIRTEEN

Finn was back to get us early in the morning, or at least I assumed it was since I had no clock and had spent the night in a dimly lit cave. He was an annoyingly chipper contrast to my gloom and doom morning attitude, but after a few sleepy protests we were back on the road as he led us through the cave system. As we walked, he expertly steered us without ever looking at a map.

"Are you sure you know where we're going?" I complained after we'd been walking for a few hours, moving faster to stand by his side. I avoided looking at Callan as I moved. We still hadn't talked since our strange conversation the night before, and I wasn't going to be the one to break the ice. "For all we know you could just be taking us in circles."

"That would be an extreme waste of my time, Rowan," Finn said as he turned us through another branch of the tunnel. "And you are not looking close enough. Use your magic and you'll be able to see the signs. We keep them hidden on the inside of the tunnels in case someone did happen to make it through our enchantments. You only think to look when you know they're there."

"I don't know how to use my magic," I told him honestly.

"I've been able to use the lightning, it seems like it wants to come out. But the magic hides from me."

"You just have to figure out your triggers. The elemental magic in us is wild, untamed. It knows no bounds and jumps at the chance to be used. Fae magic, on the other hand, is gentle. Inherent. You have to figure out what it wants and use that to coax it out of you."

"I don't even understand what that's supposed to mean," I grumbled, kicking a rock with the toe of my boot as we moved.

"Emotion. Which emotion triggers your magic? Everyone's reacts differently. Mine, for example, responds to sadness. When I was just learning how to use my magic, I learned that thinking about my mother's death worked for me."

"You think of her every time you use it?" That seemed torturous, the kind of thing that made you never want to do magic again.

"Not anymore. I've had enough years to practice that my magic and I are very in-tune. But in times that require more effort, like building these tunnels, I do."

"You said we were best friends, before I left?" He nodded with a sad smile as we walked ahead of the group. I noticed Callan hovering on the fringes, listening to conversations as we walked but not participating. Nia and Oliver trailed behind, heads bent deep in discussion about what we would do once we got to the temple.

"Yes, we were," Finn replied, his voice tinged with nostalgia. "Our families grew up with each other. One of my sisters even had a thing with Casimir. Dreadful taste if you ask me. Our betrothal was decided before we were even born; it just made sense that they forced us to spend time together.

"As we got older, we stayed friends. We got each other through a lot of messed up stuff. But I don't blame you for leaving." A pang of guilt flushed through me. I had no memory of the past, no recollection of this friendship that had clearly meant so much to him. I'd just gone and abandoned my life as a Fae, not even taking my memories with me. "Your mother never treated you well. She regularly threw you in the dungeon when you misbehaved. Which was often." I snorted at that. Some things never changed, whether I remembered them or not.

"I'm sorry, Finn. I wish I could remember."

He shook his head, his silver curls bouncing with the motion. "Don't be. If there is one thing I know about you, it's that you wouldn't have done it if you didn't think it was the only way. There was a lot of darkness in you, darkness that I don't see now. So maybe this was a good thing. You seem . . . lighter." I said nothing, not sure how to take his comment. I had no frame of reference.

We continued our journey through the labyrinth of a cave system, dimly lit tunnels casting long shadows around us. Oliver formed a fireball which he let hover along in front of us, which helped to ease the dancing shadows. I continued alongside Finn, bursting with my unasked questions until my curiosity got the better of me.

"Finn," I began, my voice a hesitant murmur, "can you tell me more about how we cursed the Queen? How did we do it?"

His cerulean eyes held a mixture of sadness and determination as he looked at me, and I could see a war waging in his mind as he decided what he wanted to say. Callan shifted in my peripherals, moving ever so slightly closer to us, and I had no doubt he was eavesdropping. "Something was different about you the day you came to find me and ask for my help. I hadn't seen you for a year, after your mother locked you up in the dungeon again. You appeared to me like a dream—looking a complete mess, might I add—and you already had the ring in hand. You wouldn't tell me where you got it, but you asked me to help you end the Queen, once and for all."

"But that didn't happen," I said, cutting off his story. "Clearly."

"No, it didn't. She was more powerful than we ever expected, and even with both of our magics combined, we were only able to curse her. The ring works like all other Fae-enchanted objects work. Off of your intentions, and using it to kill her would have killed us too."

"Maybe we should have done it anyway," I said darkly. But I meant it. The faces of the villagers we had passed swam through my mind. If we had ended her then, maybe the future would have looked much different.

"Possibly," Finn agreed. "But Casimir still would have been just as powerful, and we'd be in the same boat. With her under-ground instead of dead, at least he couldn't fully bond with the realm and gain control of the magic."

"What was the curse meant to do?"

Finn's expression grew somber. "To imprison the Queen, strip her of her powers and lock her in a place between realms—a place of eternal torment with your blood as the key. I never expected Casimir to be able to break her out."

"That was my fault." I shuddered at the gravity of our actions. I couldn't remember the weight of the choice I'd made, but it still hung over my head like a guillotine. If I hadn't erased my memo-ries, where would we be now?

MANY HOURS LATER, FINN DECIDED IT WAS TIME FOR US to make camp for the night. He'd brought us to a well-stocked outpost deep within the caves, the chamber spacious enough to accommodate us all comfortably with makeshift beds and a fire pit. I again found myself impressed at the thoroughness of his operation.

As we settled down, Finn began to set up a pot for dinner, Oliver helping him to ignite the flames under the cooking caul-dron, pulling supplies from a small chest in one corner. Soon after, a deliciously sweet aroma of fruit emerged from the pot, and our stomachs rumbled with anticipation. I dished out two bowls of the sweet stew, heading toward Callan, who sat by himself on a rock in the dimly lit corner.

I handed him the bowl, sliding in next to him on the rock, letting our thighs brush against each other just slightly. He took a few bites before he put the bowl down, leaving it to the side. "This fruit shit is getting old."

I smirked a little at his discomfort. He was the definition of a hangry man, but there was nothing I could do about it right now. "You're going to have to make do." His sour face made me giggle, and he gave me an appraising look as he watched me. I sobered up, the question I really wanted to know dancing on my tongue. Our earlier ice was broken, and he was as open as I'd ever seen him so far. *Better late than never.*

"How do you feel, now that you know Lexi is alive?" He flinched slightly when I said her name, and I tensed, waiting for him to yell or berate me for being a nosy bitch. I risked a glance at his face, searching for any sign of emotion.

His normally guarded expression softened as he stared at me, and heat bloomed in my core under his scrutiny. "It's complicated, Rowan. When I thought she was dead, I mourned her. I grieved the life we should have had before she destroyed it."

My heart ached as I listened, his unspoken pain worming its way into my chest, but I didn't dare interrupt. Even if it hurt, I wanted to hear what he had to say. I knew he would have had feelings for her, of course he did, and I had no right to want him to think any differently. But still, I did.

"Now that I know she's alive, I don't know what to feel. And I have so many goddamn questions. She's not the same Lexi I first knew, the one that I thought I loved. That person is gone. She was gone long before she killed my pack, if she was ever really there in the first place. Her actions made me question if what we had was ever really love in the first place." This was the most I'd ever heard him talk, and I hesitated, afraid to spook away the openness my question had incited within him.

"I can't even begin to imagine," I told him, deciding sympathy was my best way to keep him talking.

"I am thankful to you." My jaw dropped slightly at that. I'd never thought I'd hear words like that coming from his mouth, but I relished them. "No matter how fucked, I'd always prefer to know the truth, and now I know because of you. Lexi is somehow mixed up in all this too, and I'm determined to figure out why."

"And then what will you do?" A suspiciously light emotion like hope was beginning to blossom in my chest. It would do me no good. Even if he didn't want to be with Lexi anymore, that still didn't make him my mate. There was someone out there for me still, and it wasn't Callan. It couldn't be Callan.

"I will kill her. And make sure she stays that way. I have not forgotten that she is the one responsible for taking those young shifters' lives." He was right. They'd needed shifter hearts to help break out Queen Tantaii, in addition to my blood. And Lexi had been the rogue werewolf killing all those victims. She needed to pay for that.

A thought struck me.

"Lily told me that when one mate dies, the other one usually does too." I wasn't asking a question, but my mind was racing with the possibility of his plan. What if he was only still alive because Lexi was? If Lexi died, wouldn't Callan die too?

"I'm prepared for that eventuality," he said, not meeting my eyes. The hard set of his jaw told me there would be no arguing, so I didn't bother. Lexi wasn't dying anytime soon, and I had no right to have a say over what he chose to do with his life.

"I'm grateful too," I said finally, deciding if he could lower a wall and let me in, I could do the same. Hardening our hearts was good for our sanity, but it made for a lonely existence. "For saving me that night, and bringing me to the pack. And that you decided to come through the portal. I feel safer with you here, something familiar in this strange new world I'm trying to navigate."

"We'll get your memories back," he said, the assuredness in his voice reassuring me.

"I worry that I made the right choice, I don't think I did. I know it was to escape my brother, but I can't help wondering what I left behind. What I forgot."

"None of us can fault you for that. You did what you felt was right."

I appreciated his words, but my insecurities still gnawed at me, chewing through, layer by layer. "But what if I missed out on something important? What if I left someone behind who needed me?"

Callan reached out and gently touched my hand, his warm fingers wrapping around my cold ones gently, sending shivers down my spine. "You can't change the past, Rowan. All you can do is work toward the future. I think we could both probably learn from that lesson."

I peeked a glance at him, shadows dancing across his handsome features. My heart pounded in my chest as he turned to look at me, the tension between us deepening until I could almost taste it. Our eyes locked, and I looked away quickly. He squeezed my hand, and my head turned, almost against my own volition.

Our eyes locked again, and this time, I didn't look away. There was a vulnerability in Callan's gaze, a flicker of something intense and raw. It mirrored my own gaze, and I couldn't ignore the growing tension between us any longer. My mouth moved before my brain could catch up, bulldozing its way through my life like it usually did.

"What is this?" My voice was barely above a whisper, and if it wasn't for the slight widening of his eyes, I would have thought I never spoke. "Don't tell me you don't feel it too."

Callan swallowed hard, his eyes never leaving mine. "Rowan, I . . ." He trailed off, seemingly at a loss for words. I took a deep breath, my heart pounding in my chest as I waited for him to speak. He moved his hand, slowly sliding from my arm to my cheek, his burning touch gentle as it feathered my skin. "We can't. And you know why."

We were close enough that I could feel the heat radiating from

Callan's body, and I longed to bridge the gap between us and crush my lips over his. There was no Mating Moon this time, no outside influence to the heat I was feeling. This was all me, and all targeted toward Callan.

"What if I don't care?" I whispered.

Callan's eyes were hooded pits by this time, his turmoil evident as he fought his instincts. He closed his eyes briefly, and when he opened them again, his steel mask was back in place as he dropped his hand from my face. "I do. I've told you before. As much as I would love to take you to my tent and have my way with you, I've done my time. This would only end in heartache when you eventually find your mate."

Anger flared in me as his walls fully snapped back into place, coldness the only thing I could garner from his expression. Without another word, I pushed off from the rock and stormed away.

This time, he was the one left staring at my back.

CHAPTER FOURTEEN

O liver cleared his throat, interrupting our seemingly endless march through the cave system. "You know, Rowan," he said with a wry grin, "since we have all this quality time together while we're trudging through the tunnels, it might be a good opportunity to work on your magical abilities."

I rolled my eyes and shot back, my tone dripping with sarcasm, "Oh, absolutely, Oliver. Because nothing screams 'fun' like practicing magic in a dark, damp cave."

"Well, my dear, mastering your magic could prove invaluable on this journey."

I sighed dramatically, feigning reluctance. "Fine, fine, let's get this over with. Teach me your magical ways, oh wise and ancient one."

Oliver raised an eyebrow, his lips curling into an amused smile. "Very well, young apprentice. First, we'll work on your lightning powers."

I nodded, trying to muster some enthusiasm. "Great, that's been going so well for me so far."

Oliver chuckled again, then turned serious as he began his instruction. "Focus on the energy within you, Rowan. Feel it, like a crackling storm just waiting to be unleashed. Now, visualize that energy gathering in your hands."

I closed my eyes and took a deep breath, attempting to follow his guidance. A moment later, I opened my eyes and shrugged. "I don't feel anything. Maybe my lightning is on vacation. Off to go start a storm or something."

Oliver's laughter echoed in the cave, and he shook his head. "Patience, my dear. Rome wasn't built in a day, and neither are lightning-wielding halflings."

I smirked at his response. "Alright, alright, I'll keep trying. But only because you're so persuasive."

As we continued through the cave, Oliver patiently guided me through the basics of controlling my lightning powers. Sparks occasionally crackled from my fingertips, but I struggled to maintain any real control.

After a particularly frustrating attempt, I grumbled, "You know, Oliver, I'm starting to think lightning isn't my thing. Maybe I should stick to something less. . . electrifying."

Oliver patted my shoulder with a reassuring smile. "Don't give up just yet, Rowan. We all have our unique talents waiting to be discovered."

I sighed and decided to switch the subject. "Alright, magic master, what's next on the agenda?"

Oliver looked thoughtful for a moment before suggesting, "How about learning to see basic magic? It'll help you detect signs and pathways hidden by enchantments in the tunnel system."

I raised an eyebrow. "That didn't work very well when we tried the water thing."

"You're absolutely right, exactly why we should keep working on it. Now, focus on your surroundings, but instead of seeing the physical cave walls, try to see the magic that conceals them."

I did as instructed, squinting at the cave walls as though I could see beyond their rocky surface. After a few moments, I furrowed my brow in frustration. "All I see are rocks, Oliver. Plain, old, ugly rocks."

"Hey!" Finn exclaimed, "I worked hard on these rocks."

"It takes time and practice, Rowan. Magic sight isn't something that develops overnight. Keep trying, and you'll get the hang of it. Eventually it'll be something you can just switch on and off, like putting on a pair of glasses."

I sighed, feeling a tad bit defeated. "Why does everything magical have to be so complicated?"

Oliver placed a comforting hand on my shoulder. "Because, my dear, the most extraordinary things in life are often worth the effort."

We continued, my sarcastic remarks and Oliver's patient guidance creating an odd, yet oddly effective, dynamic. The rest of the group trailed along, Callan keeping a watchful eye even though I was doing my best to not look at him.

As we advanced on our journey through the winding tunnels, I kept honing my magical skills. With Oliver's guidance, I attempted to call upon my lightning powers more consistently. I'd stand at various points along our route, focusing on the stormy energy inside me, and attempt to channel it into the palms of my hands. The results were often unpredictable, and I was still far from mastering this newfound ability.

"Come on, Rowan," Oliver encouraged me. "You've got the spark in you, quite literally. You just need to learn how to control it."

I rolled my eyes at his pun but continued to concentrate. Sparks flew from my fingertips a few times, but they were more like wild, erratic fireworks than a controlled display of power. One such burst of lightning almost struck Oliver, but he skillfully dodged it.

"Watch out, Oliver! Lightning-thrower on the loose!" I

quipped, trying to infuse some humor into my clumsy attempts so they wouldn't notice my reddening cheeks.

Oliver chuckled, unharmed by my electrical mishap. He was fast growing at me, given he was the only one who laughed at my lame jokes. "Don't worry, I've had worse."

"How did you learn to master your magic so well?" I asked him as we made camp one night.

"My mother mostly. She was amazing. You remind me a lot of her actually," he said. "She was a witch and my father a distant air royal. She's been long gone for many years now, but she was incredibly powerful. Much more powerful than my father."

"Do you miss her?" I asked him, and then immediately regretted the question. Of course he would miss her.

"I miss the idea of her," he said finally, taking the time to really contemplate my question. "When you live as long as we do, it's easy to forget those we started our lives with. Being a halfling has incredible benefits, and I wouldn't change it for the world, but sometimes I do wonder what it would have been like to be only a witch and live a normal lifespan."

"You spent a lot of time imprisoned by the Queen, didn't you?"

"More than I would wish on even my greatest enemies. She is a cruel person. Olette knew that better than anyone. I know you have a lot of questions on why you did what you did, but your mother put you through a lot. I don't doubt that you did what was right. And I, for one, will be eternally grateful that you freed me from that prison."

He reached over, giving my knee a fatherly pat, and I gave hm a genuine smile. Something told me neither Olette nor I ever had even a semblance of a paternal relationship until Oliver. I liked the older man, and I'd grown to trust him.

"For what it's worth," I told him, "I'd do it again in a heartbeat."

OVER THE REMAINING TWO DAYS OF OUR JOURNEY, I slowly began to gain a modicum of control. The lightning bolts became less wild, and I managed to direct them toward specific targets, albeit with limited accuracy. While I couldn't conjure a raging storm just yet, I was getting better, and that gave me hope.

Aside from my magic training, I also learned to see basic magical signs and pathways hidden within the tunnels. With his knowledgeable expanse of magic sight, Finn took the lead in teaching me this skill. He would pause occasionally, pointing out subtle cues, such as faint glimmers or shifts in the air. These signs revealed concealed paths, enchantments, and potential dangers lurking in the dark recesses of the cave system I hadn't expected. By the end of the journey, it was a lot like snapping glasses into place.

"Magic, my dear Rowan, is like a secret language," Finn explained one day as we walked. As we spent more time together, we'd settled into a mildly flirty banter, but it was just fun and I think we both knew that. He was gorgeous, but he didn't light a fire in me the way Callan did. "Learn to read the signs, and you'll find a wealth of knowledge hidden in plain sight."

"Secret language, huh?" I quirked an eyebrow. I'd begun to realize why we would have been friends. We had a similar sense of humor, and he was outgoing, which was something I'd come to realize I liked in a friend, someone who could pull me out of my more withdrawn nature.

Callan, on the other hand, remained a brooding presence on our journey. After our last conversation, an awkward tension had settled between us again. We spoke only when necessary, and his steely gaze rarely met mine. Yet, I couldn't help but feel his eyes on me when he thought I wasn't looking, and the way they lingered.

Still, I often found myself stealing glances at him. He moved with a fluid grace, every step deliberate and powerful. His strong, sinewy muscles flexed beneath the fabric of his clothing, and his chiseled features remained set in an unwavering mask of determination.

I couldn't deny the attraction I felt toward him, and it frustrated me to no end. Callan was the embodiment of mystery and allure, a complex enigma I longed to unravel. But he had his mate, Lexi, and he'd made it clear he wouldn't entertain anything beyond friendship with me, even if he wasn't sure of his original feelings for Lexi.

One evening, when we set up camp within the underground outpost Finn had created, Nia approached me.

"Rowan," Nia said, her voice carrying the weight of her status as one of the bonded, "may I speak with you for a moment?"

I nodded, intrigued by the request, and followed her a short distance away from the campfire. She glanced around to ensure our conversation remained private.

"I sense that you have a strong affinity for magic," Nia began, her eyes penetrating my soul. "It is a rare gift, one that can be a formidable force for good. But it can also be a double-edged sword."

I raised an eyebrow, curiosity piqued. "What do you mean?"

Nia hesitated for a moment before continuing. "I've been observing your progress. You have potential to be even stronger than I think any of us realize, but you need to take it more seriously. Remember your responsibility."

I frowned, not entirely sure where she was going with this. "Responsibility? To whom?"

Nia's gaze softened, revealing a hint of vulnerability beneath her composed exterior. "To yourself, and to those who depend on you. You are capable of wielding immense power, but you must learn to control it without letting it consume you. Your mother and Casimir both fell victim to the wrong kind of mindset."

I nodded my understanding. "I won't make the same mistakes they did."

Nia's expression relaxed, and a small, genuine smile tugged at the corners of her lips. "I have faith in you, Rowan. You have a rare spirit, one that can unite and inspire others. You just don't realize it yet."

Her words left me both awed and humbled. Nia had seen something within me that I had yet to fully grasp, and even though I barely knew her, I found myself looking up to her. She was strong, with a sense of self and duty that I admired. Something I may have even been a bit jealous of. As we returned to the campfire, I couldn't help but feel a renewed sense of purpose. I wanted to make these people proud.

For myself, for my friend, and for my realms.

The final leg of our journey brought us closer to our destination—the cave exit that was a mere two miles away from the Primoris Temple. The anticipation in the air was palpable, a mixture of hope and uncertainty. The prospect of regaining my memories was both exhilarating and terrifying.

As we finally approached the exit, I took one last look at the winding tunnels that had been our home for the past few days. I had learned so much during this journey, not only about magic but also about myself and the people who now surrounded me.

I was ready to face this head-on.

CHAPTER FIFTEEN

E merging from the confines of the tunnel, the group was met with a breathtaking view of Primoris City. The ornate buildings and winding streets stretched out before them, with the Queen's menacing castle casting a shadow over the city's heart. In the distance, a majestic temple stood tall, its spires reaching for the heavens.

I squinted, trying to find any fragment of memory within me. "Does the city always look this . . . theatrical?" I smirked, pointing towards the Queen's castle.

Nia's blue hair shimmered in the sunlight. "It's been said the Queen has a flair for the dramatic," she replied, water droplets orbiting her hand as her anxiety grew. It seemed that might be *her* emotional trigger, which I found fascinating given how composed she always seemed to be.

Oliver snorted. "That's one way to put it."

The brief moment of levity was interrupted as a lightning bolt fractured the horizon, and a pit of dread burst to life inside of me. In its wake stood Cas, every bit the picture of impeccable douche-iness, with his blonde hair tousled by the electric aura surrounding him.

Beside him, Lexi's scar was a glaring testament to her violent past with Callan. Her eyes bore into us with malice, no love remaining in her eyes as she saw her former mate. Ever the enigmatic witch, Roxy scanned the group with a superior air, her dark gaze resting momentarily on Oliver with a sneer. A menacing group of the snake-like naga flanked them.

Callan's muscles tensed, the panther within him growling softly. Callan's eyes locked onto Lexi's with an icy precision, his Alpha power already brimming under the surface. We all gripped our weapons and magic tighter. A fight was going to be the only way we got out of this situation.

Lexi's eyes danced with a hint of madness as she leaned in slightly. "Tell me, Callan, do you miss me?" A snarl erupted on his face but he said nothing, angling his body to be half a step ahead of me, blocking my view of her.

I turned my attention to Cas, who was inching closer, and I took an involuntary step back.

Cas tilted his head with a knowing smile. "Still running, little sister?"

I flashed a defiant grin, giving him my middle finger and projecting a confidence I didn't possess.

As the two groups faced off, the nagas slithered forth, their green-scaled forms reflecting the sunlight menacingly. The venomous sheen on their weapons served as a deadly warning.

Fire kindled around Oliver's fists. "We need a strategy."

I shrugged. "Don't die?"

Cas stepped forward, radiating confidence. "It ends here, sister. Give me the ring."

Adrenaline surged through me as Cas lunged at me with a crackling bolt of lightning in his hand. I dodged to the side, narrowly avoiding his attack, but the rush of energy brushed against my arm, leaving a searing sensation in its wake. Pain radiated from the burn, but I couldn't let it distract me.

Oliver rushed to my side, flames dancing in his palms as he

aimed them at Cas. "Stay back, Casimir!" Oliver's voice held a warning edge.

Cas smirked, his eyes wild with power. "You've always been too soft, Oliver." With a flick of his wrist, he sent another arc of lightning my way.

I concentrated on my newfound abilities, gathering the energy within me. With a burst of effort, I managed to redirect the incoming bolt, sending it crackling harmlessly into the ground. I wasn't as skilled as Cas, but I was learning fast.

Meanwhile, Callan and Lexi were locked in a fierce struggle, both in their animal forms. Their snarls and growls filled the air as they circled each other, claws and teeth flashing.

Roxy and Finn engaged in a mesmerizing dance of magic within the cavern, each weaving their unique powers to create a dazzling display. Finn, his air magic swirling around him like an invisible tornado, launched gusts of wind and razor-sharp currents toward Roxy. She countered with intricate spells, conjuring barriers of shimmering energy that deflected the aerial onslaught.

Nia, with her power over water, faced off against the naga. Her mastery over the water gave her an advantage, and she summoned tendrils of liquid from the ground to bind and restrain the serpentine creatures. They hissed and writhed, their venomous fangs snapping dangerously.

Cas was growing more relentless with each passing moment. Oliver kept him at bay with his fire magic, but I knew I would need to contribute more to the fight in order for us to get out of here alive. I could smell Cas's electrical energy, a metallic tang in the air as he sent blast after blast.

I waited for the right moment. As Cas prepared another lightning strike, I sensed the charge building up. At the last second, I ducked and rolled to the side, narrowly avoiding the deadly bolt as he launched it at my head. With a surge of energy, I let loose a frazzled burst of lightning, aiming it directly at Cas. He yelped in pain as it struck him, sending him tumbling backward.

Oliver seized the opportunity, surrounding Cas with a ring of fire, trapping him momentarily. We had the upper hand, but I knew Cas wasn't going to stay down for long. If he were that easy to beat, he never would have kept the throne in the first place.

Curses flew as he struggled within the fiery circle that Oliver had conjured. He was trapped, but not beaten. Lightning crackled around him as he fought to break free, searching for a weakness. He blasted at the flames, and I was surprised to see they never left the circle, magic mixing with the flames in a glittering shimmer. Anger burned as he looked out toward us.

"Rowan!" Oliver called to me, his voice laced with urgency, and I turned my attention back to him. "Keep him occupied. I'll finish this!"

I nodded, my heart pounding as I faced my brother once more. He'd gone silent, his eyes closed. Was he accepting his defeat? That seemed *highly* unlikely.

Gathering more energy, I kept my powers at the surface, ready to strike out if needed.

Suddenly, Casimir's form shimmered, and he vanished in a burst of lightning from the sky, leaving nothing but a smoky residue behind. He had teleported himself out of the fiery circle.

"Damn it," I muttered, scanning the cave for any sign of him. "I didn't know we could do that."

Then, without warning, Casimir reappeared behind me, a malevolent grin on his face. Before I could react, he sent a surge of electricity through the ground, creating a shockwave that knocked me off my feet. I cried out in pain as my body convulsed from the electric current.

"Rowan!" Callan's voice echoed in the distance.

But Cas wasn't done. He approached, his eyes filled with a twisted delight. "You were always the weaker one," he sneered. "Too compassionate, too soft. An abomination. Just give me what I want. You are only prolonging the inevitable."

Summoning all the strength I could muster, I focused on the

lightning within me, gathering more. With a defiant burst, I sent a torrent of electricity toward Cas, catching him by surprise. He screamed as the lightning surged through him, and his body convulsed.

Gasping for breath, I forced myself to my feet, my vision still blurred from the shockwave. Cas laid on the ground, twitching. He was injured, but I couldn't let my guard down.

Oliver appeared by my side, concern etched across his face. "Are you alright, Rowan?"

I nodded, panting heavily. "I'll live. But we need to finish this."

Nia continued to manipulate the water with finesse, creating a swirling vortex that entrapped the nagas, rendering them momentarily immobile. Her concentration was evident as she struggled to maintain control over the elemental forces. "We need to go, now!" she shouted over the chaos.

Callan, still engaged in a fierce struggle with Lexi, understood the urgency. His panther form lunged at Lexi, teeth bared, momentarily pushing her back and keeping her from pursuing us.

Oliver's flames blazed brighter as he created a wall of fire to deter Roxy, jumping in to help Finn with the powerful witch. "We'll hold them off! Rowan, get to the temple, you'll be protected inside!"

Finn conjured a swirling gust of wind that created a temporary barrier between our group and our adversaries. "Move! We'll be right behind you," he urged.

I ran. Finn's air power now coupled with Oliver's fire as they created a fearsome wall that bought me precious time. The temple loomed in the distance, its grandeur becoming more apparent with every step. I pushed myself harder, my adrenaline-fueled legs carrying me closer to safety. If we could just get there, we'd be momentarily safe on the inside. Cracks of lightning burst overhead, and I knew Cas would come in hot.

The sounds of battle echoed behind me, and I risked a glance, eyes widening as I saw the elemental shield flare brightly. My friends turned to follow me, Callan's panther form breaking ahead. The temple's massive doors grew larger in my vision, and intricate runes weaving a mesmerizing pattern on the stone.

With a final burst of speed, I reached the temple doors.

Chapter Sixteen

E ntering the Primoris Temple was like stepping into another world—a world of tranquility and ancient magic that seemed to embrace us the moment we crossed the threshold. The temple's polished marble floors glowed with a soft, ethereal light, and the air was filled with the soothing scent of blooming flowers.

It was a jarring contrast to the chaos that brewed outside as my friends ran in behind me. I scanned their faces, grateful to see everyone had made it in. Callan's panther brushed closely by my side.

'Are you hurt?'

"I'm fine," I responded aloud, severing our connection by walking ahead, toward the back of the temple.

As I ventured further in, my friends followed closely behind, their footsteps echoing in the grand chamber as we entered. The atmosphere was thick with an almost tangible sense of enchantment. It felt alive, full of power.

The intricate carvings adorning the walls depicted stories of ancient times and forgotten legends. The temple's magic seemed to resonate within each of us, drawing us deeper into its depths and filling us with a sense of rightness that I couldn't explain.

I couldn't help but pause, marveling at the breathtaking surroundings. It was as if the temple itself held a secret, an answer to the questions that had plagued me for so long. I glanced back at my friends, a mixture of excitement and trepidation churning within me. I was so close to getting my memories back.

A willowy woman approached us, her pointed ears and wise demeanor a testament to the agelessness of this place. "Welcome to the Primoris Temple," she greeted us, her voice soft and melodious. "I am Vailia, the guardian of this sacred place. How may I assist you today?" Doubt consumed my mind, and I didn't know how to respond. Vailia, as if attuned to my inner conflict, offered a reassuring smile. "Do not worry, dear child. You have a special purpose to fulfill here. We thought you might come."

I raised an eyebrow, my curiosity piqued. "Special purpose? Does that come with a manual?"

Vailia's laughter was like a gentle breeze rustling through leaves. "Not a manual, but guidance, if you're lucky. Follow me. Your friends will need to stay here."

With a graceful turn, Vailia led our group deeper into the temple. I glanced at my friends, silently hoping they understood my need to explore the secrets of this place. The last thing I saw as we rounded the corner was Callan, his glare blazing a hole in her head.

THE BATHHOUSE WITHIN THE PRIMORIS TEMPLE WAS A vision of serenity. The walls were adorned with intricate mosaics of mystical creatures, and the room was filled with the delicate fragrance of exotic flowers. Vailia guided me towards a large, sunken marble pool filled with clear, sparkling water.

"You must cleanse yourself before entering the presence of the goddess," Vailia explained. "To rid yourself of any corrupt impurities."

I nodded, doing my best not to get offended that she thought I had corrupt impurities. "How did you know I was coming?"

Vailia's response was cryptic, her gaze distant. "The whispers of the realms carry secrets, Rowan. The river of time is ever-flowing. You have walked these halls, but you have also been a stranger to them."

Her words were as enigmatic as the temple itself, leaving me with more questions than answers. It was frustrating, but I couldn't deny the anticipation that stirred within me.

I began to disrobe, slipping into the refreshing waters of the pool. The coolness enveloped my skin, washing away the grime and weariness from the battles I'd faced. My fingers trailed through the water, and I couldn't help but wonder about the mysteries hidden within this sacred place.

As I bathed, Vailia remained by my side, her presence both comforting and unsettling. Her eyes watched me with a knowing gaze, as if she could peer into the depths of my very soul. I decided to press her further, desperate for any clues about my past.

"Will I be able to get my memories back?" I asked cautiously.

Vailia's smile was gentle. "Memories are like leaves on the surface of a river. Some are carried away by the current, while others remain submerged, waiting to resurface."

What? I think Vailia had cleansed herself a few too many times.

Either way, I suspected the truth, even if I didn't want to admit it. When I was Olette, the unwanted daughter of Queen Tantaii, I had come to this temple in search of answers. I had sought the goddess's guidance, hoping to escape my miserable life and start anew. But the goddess had shown me the path to becoming Rowan, and I had willingly left behind the memories of Olette and the painful existence I had endured.

I had chosen to forget, and I knew I should trust that decision given I'd been the one to make it. But now, standing in the bathhouse of the Primoris Temple, I couldn't help but wonder if I had made the right choice.

Once I had finished cleansing myself, Vailia guided me to a pristine chamber with flowing white curtains. It felt like stepping into a dream. In the center of the room, an ornate mirror framed in gold and adorned with shimmering gems awaited me.

"This mirror is a portal to the presence of the goddess Prim," Vailia explained. "Step through it, and you will find yourself in the sacred chamber."

I nodded, my heart pounding with a mix of anticipation and anxiety. I glanced back at the mirror, my reflection wavering in its surface. It was now or never.

I took a deep breath.

I stepped through the ornate mirror, my surroundings shifting instantly. The new chamber I found myself in was unlike anything I had ever seen. It radiated with an ethereal light, and the air hummed with an ancient power that was almost suffocating. Being here felt wrong, like I wasn't worthy enough to even exist.

"Okay, Rowan, don't freak out," I muttered to myself, the nervousness bubbling up and making me babble. "You've got this. Just talk to the goddess like you're chatting with a friend."

As I turned around, I was met with a breathtaking sight. The goddess Prim stood before me, her presence commanding the entire chamber. She appeared as if she had materialized from the very essence of magic itself. Her skin seemed to shimmer with an inner light, and her eyes held the wisdom of countless ages.

"Hey there," I greeted, a half-nervous smile tugging at my lips. "Nice place you've got here. Very 'goddess-y.'"

The goddess Prim regarded me with a serene smile, her voice a gentle melody. "Greetings, Rowan, seeker of answers. I am pleased that you have returned."

I couldn't help but fidget under her piercing gaze. "Yeah, well, life's full of surprises, you know? So, I'm here because, um, I need to find my memories. The ones I sort of . . . hid from myself." I paused, realizing I was probably babbling again.

The goddess's eyes held a depth of understanding. "I know of your request, Rowan, but I must be honest with you. The memories you seek, they cannot be returned."

My heart sank, and I felt a lump forming in my throat. "What? But . . . I thought you could help me. I thought you had the power to bring them back."

Prim's voice remained gentle but resolute. "I do possess great power, but some things are beyond even my abilities. Magic has to have balance, just as life does. The memories you hid away, you did so for a reason. To protect yourself, perhaps. To move forward in your life. I can't really say. But it doesn't change the fact that I cannot bring them back."

Tears welled up in my eyes, and I blinked them back furiously. "But I need to know. I need to remember who I was, what I did. It's important."

The goddess's ethereal form seemed to shimmer with sympathy. "I understand your desire, Rowan, but the past is not always a kind place. Sometimes, it is better left undisturbed. I can offer you guidance, but I cannot grant the memories you seek."

I swallowed hard, trying to process the weight of her words. "So, there's no way? No way at all to get them back?"

Prim's expression remained sorrowful. "I am sorry, Rowan. Some things are lost to us forever."

Devastation washed over me, and I couldn't hold back the tears any longer. It was as if a part of me had been shattered irreparably. I had come all this way, held onto hope so tightly, only to have it slip through my fingers like sand.

My shoulders slumped, and I whispered in a broken voice, "I don't understand. Why? Why did I do this?"

Prim's response was filled with compassion as she reached out to touch my cheek. "Sometimes, my dear, the pain of the past is too great to bear. And sometimes, it is our own hearts that protect us from that pain. Trust that your journey is not in vain."

I nodded, my vision blurred by tears, and I knew that no matter what, I would have to find a way to accept the truth, to move forward, even if I couldn't unlock my memories. This didn't make my memories go away.

As I wiped away my tears, the goddess Prim extended a delicate hand towards me, her fingers holding a small, sealed envelope made of pristine parchment. "Rowan," she said softly, "I cannot grant you your memories, but perhaps this will bring you some solace."

I accepted the envelope, my curiosity piqued, and I examined the elegant script that adorned its surface. "What is this?" I asked, my voice trembling.

Prim's eyes bore into mine, a deep sadness within them. "It is a letter, written by someone who once stood where you stand now."

My heart pounded in my chest as I carefully broke the seal and unfolded the parchment.

Dear Rowan,

If you're reading this, it means you've embarked on a journey I had hoped you would never have to take. Our life, shrouded in a mother's cruelty, was far from kind. We were the unfortunate offspring of Queen Tantaii, bearing the weight of her malevolence, and a rabbit shifter, who I named you after.

Engar Rowan. I think it's important for you to know that, so he's never completely forgotten. She would enjoy that too much.

In my quest, I joined forces with Finn to curse the Queen and imprison her beneath the earth's surface. It was a bold move, and it wasn't enough. I know that now. Even the both of us didn't have enough power to kill her, Rowan, and I couldn't attain it on my own. So we cursed her instead.

And then I ran.

Our mother locked up our halfling abilities years ago, at the first sign that I was anything but Fae. She hates us. She hates anyone who isn't her, really, but especially me. I wasn't strong enough to beat her, and I'm not strong enough to beat Cas.

But I hope that you are, when the time is right.

Find yourself. Find our heritage.

The ring holds the answers. You know the one I speak of—the very object I concealed, even from our own memories. You must find it, before Casimir does. Erasing our memories is a huge risk, but I can't let it fall into the wrong hands should I get caught. There is too much at stake. Hopefully, Prim's words hold true, and the ring will be safe. I hope you can forgive me for this choice.

Its location remains my secret, and I won't disclose it in this letter, for fear it might fall into the wrong hands. While I doubt the Queen could extinguish Prim's life, I've learned never to underestimate her. You would do well to remember the same.

I will leave you with this. Trust your heart, and your instincts. You have them for a reason.

-Olette

My hands trembled as I read the letter, the weight of its words settling over me like a heavy shroud. Olette had made a choice, hidden the ring away, even from herself.

Prim's voice brought me back to the present. "Before you ask, I cannot tell you where the ring is."

"What? Why not? She made it sound like—"

"Not because I don't want to, child," she soothed, a calming energy settling through me as she explained. "But because I don't know where it is. No one does."

I nodded, clutching the letter to my chest. I would find the ring. I could do it. The letter was a piece of my past, a glimpse into the life I had hidden from myself.

"I've cast a spell to send your adversaries away, my dear," Prim called as she started to waver in the air, her form losing focus. Her tone carrying a hint of sassy reproach. "It will be a few hours before they've realized what happened. Wouldn't want any bloodstains marring my sacred abode."

Chapter Seventeen

As I stood in the sacred chamber, the weight of Prim's words sank in like a stone, turning my hopes to despair. The realization that I would never retrieve my stolen memories hit me like a wave, threatening to drown me, pulling me under.

I couldn't bear to face the group now, not with the disappointment welling up inside me. They depended on me, and all I had to go on was a cryptic-ass clue that didn't make any sense. So, for the first time since I first shifted in the woods at the Clover pack, I let the transformation overtake me, sinking into the wave of my shifter powers. My body contorted, and in moments, I was no longer the woman they knew but instead a small, white, bushy-tailed rabbit.

Without a second glance, I hopped away, my furry paws barely making a sound on the pristine temple floor. My heart pounded as I moved silently past my friends, who remained unaware of the escape plan I was trying to enact.

Or so I thought.

As I reached the threshold of the chamber, a low growl rumbled through the air, sending shivers down my spine. I turned to see Callan, his panther form sleek and powerful, his eyes fixed on me with a mix of concern and determination. He had caught the faintest scent of my rabbit form, and there was no deceiving his keen senses.

In an instant, I was off, darting through the doorway and into the forest beyond. My little bunny legs carried me faster than any ordinary rabbit could hope to go. Oliver's shouts followed me as I sped away, but I was determined to outpace them. I was headed nowhere in particular, just needing to create space between me and my problems.

The world became a blur of green and brown as I raced through the woods, my heart pounding in my chest. I was a streak of white against the backdrop of nature, my instincts guiding me deeper into the forest as I dove and twisted onto paths I knew Callan wouldn't be able to follow with his much larger size.

I couldn't afford to look back. The disappointment of not regaining my memories still weighed heavily on me, but right now, all that mattered was putting distance between me and the temple, and my persistent pursuers.

I came to a panting stop in what seemed like a secluded patch of the forest. My little rabbit heart raced, and I couldn't help but reflect on the weight of disappointment that hung over me like a storm cloud. Not being able to reclaim my stolen memories felt like a crushing blow, a cruel twist of fate.

I sank down onto my fluffy haunches and let out a long, weary sigh. *Well, isn't this just fantastic?* I tittered to myself.

Where the fuck was this ring? It was as if I had played a twisted game of hide and seek with my own memories, and I was losing at every turn. Guilt gnawed at me as I considered the implications of not having that ring. The realm suffered under my family's rule, their indifference allowing towns to languish in poverty while they reveled in their opulence.

I knew that they would never stop coming for me, never stop chasing me. It was a relentless pursuit that showed no mercy. I worried about the safety of my pack back in Clover, especially about Lily and Wolfe. What would happen to them if

Cas came for them? He didn't know any of this; he thought I had the ring.

The only thing standing between the Queen and carrying out her plot.

As I sat there, surrounded by the comforting embrace of the forest, I knew I couldn't stay in this melancholic reverie for long. There was too much happening, and even if I couldn't regain my memories, I had a duty to protect those I cared about and try and figure out where I hid the ring.

I was alone in the forest, my thoughts echoing in the solitude when suddenly, I felt a warm touch on my furry back. It was Callan, his panther form melding with mine, and I could sense the concern in his touch. *'Rowan, are you crazy? Why did you run off like that? You could have gotten yourself killed.'*

I felt a pang of guilt as I responded, my thoughts reaching out to him in the way only shifters could. *'I needed some space,'* I admitted, my mental voice filled with a mixture of sadness and frustration. *'I couldn't face them, not after what Prim said.'*

Callan's presence in my mind was a comforting one, and he tried to soothe my unease. *'You can't get your memories back.'* His mental voice was calm and stoic, practically reading my mind. *'We'll figure this out together.'*

I nuzzled against his panther form, feeling the warmth of his fur against mine. I shouldn't have let myself, but I couldn't resist. *'I know,'* I replied softly. *'But I just . . . I don't have any answers, Callan. I don't know where the ring is, and I feel so guilty that I can't stop my family from causing more harm.'*

Callan's mental touch remained steady as he said, *'We'll find a way. We won't rest until this is over. I promise.'*

With a deep breath, I pushed away my worries, focusing on the present moment. *'I just needed a moment to catch my breath,'* I admitted, feeling a bit more composed. *'Let's head back before they get too worried.'*

Callan withdrew his touch, and together, we began the journey back to where our friends waited, their shouts of concern echoing through the forest. As we made our way through the dense undergrowth, I couldn't help but marvel at the fact that I had finally managed to shift on my own. It was a small victory amidst the chaos, but it was enough to give me a glimmer of hope for what lay ahead.

WE REVERTED TO OUR HUMAN FORMS, THE LINGERING adrenaline from our earlier encounter still pulsing through our veins, quickly dressing. My dagger was securely fastened to my hip. We had retreated to the familiar depths of the caves, with no further attacks or threats lurking in the shadows. It appeared that Prim had indeed fulfilled her promise by sending our enemies away, and Finn had used his magic to reinforce the tunnel for added security.

Seated in a circle, we collectively pondered our next course of action. Nia, Oliver, Callan, Finn, and I engaged in a forlorn discussion, tossing ideas back and forth.

My frustration was evident in my voice as I spoke first. "We need to find that damned ring, but where do we even start? It could be hidden anywhere in this realm, and we don't have a single lead."

"It could be in either realm, even. We just don't know," Nia added.

Oliver nodded, his thoughtful expression mirroring my own concerns. "Directly confronting the Queen and Cas would be too risky. They have an entire army at their disposal, and now they're aware of our presence."

Callan's gaze was fixed on the cave floor as he weighed our options. "We can't stay here, Rowan," he finally stated, his voice somber. "This realm holds nothing for you, especially now that we know retrieving your memories is impossible. You're safer on the mortal side, where we have backup."

I let out a heavy sigh, coming to terms with the painful reality. Our initial mission had crumbled, and the peril we were in stared me in the face. "So, what's the plan?"

Oliver leaned back against the cave wall, his expression pensive. "Maybe it's time to consider returning through the portal to the Clover pack," he suggested. "We can assess the situation there, regroup, and determine our next steps."

Although it pained me to think about leaving the Faerie realm behind, it did seem like the most sensible choice. "Perhaps it's safer for us on the mortal side, at least for now," I reluctantly admitted. Guilt at leaving the people who lived so harshly to fend for themselves still wormed its way immediately into my heart.

Our group huddled together in the dimly lit cave, the decision to return to the Clover pack weighing heavily on our minds. I looked around at my Fae companions, "You don't all have to come back with me. I know you have places to protect and people depending on you."

Nia, her striking blue hair shimmering faintly in the cave's ambient glow, was the first to speak. "I have my stronghold to oversee, but I can spare a few days," she said, her voice filled with determination. "Aura assures me that it's safe and secure."

Finn, his air magic faintly swirling around him, glanced around the cave with an intrigued expression. "I've never been to the mortal realm," he mused. "Plus, I want to do everything I can to help you, Rowan. I mean that."

Oliver, always the steadfast companion, nodded in agreement. "Where Rowan goes, I go," he affirmed, his voice unwavering.

I couldn't help but feel a swell of gratitude for my friends and their willingness to stay on the journey with me.

CHAPTER EIGHTEEN

O liver's hands moved with a practiced grace, weaving an intricate pattern in the air before him. His fingers danced through the motions, and as he did, a subtle hum of energy filled the cavern, making the very air vibrate with anticipation. I watched in awe as the circle he traced began to shimmer, its edges glowing with a soft, otherworldly light.

The circular portal gradually expanded, revealing a glimpse of what lay beyond. Through the portal, I could see the rusted iron gates of the Clover pack, a familiarity settling into my bones and excitement brewing.

We had made our decision to return to the Clover pack, but now that the portal stood open before us, there was a moment of hesitation—a lingering doubt about what we might find on the other side.

It was Callan who broke the silence, his voice gentle yet resolute. "Rowan, you first," he said, stepping aside to allow me to approach the portal.

His words carried a weight of history. The last time we had had the opportunity to go through a portal, I never arrived on the other side. He raised an eyebrow at me and crossed his arms, looking about ready to pick me up and toss me through.

I didn't hesitate. I took a deep breath, my heart pounding. With a determined step, I crossed the threshold of the portal.

The transition was as swift and disorienting as it was last time. It felt as though I had been pulled through a vortex, the world around me blurring and distorting before snapping back into focus. When I looked around, I found myself standing on familiar ground, within the concealed boundaries of the Clover pack.

The rusted iron gates greeted me as they always had. The forest beyond them stretched out, an untamed wilderness. But there was something different about the world I saw now, both strange and oddly familiar.

Nia, Finn, and Oliver emerged from the portal one by one, their expressions mirroring my own sense of disorientation. The Fae among us, Nia and Finn, looked around with a mixture of curiosity and bewilderment. To them, the mortal realm was a wondrous and alien place, a contrast to the Faerie realm from which they hailed.

The air felt different here, carrying scents and sensations that were unique to the mortal realm. The earth beneath our feet was solid, and the trees stood tall and imposing, their leaves rustling in the breeze.

Callan, ever the guardian, stepped through the portal last. His gaze locked onto mine, and I could see the unspoken relief in his eyes. We had crossed the threshold together this time, and I was here, standing beside him.

As the portal behind us closed with a soft, ethereal hum, a sense of determination settled over our group. I had returned to the mortal realm, to the place I called home, and I was ready to face whatever challenges awaited us.

Our journey had brought us full circle, back to the heart of our pack, and I was scared shitless that I wouldn't be able to keep them safe.

LILY PRACTICALLY LAUNCHED HERSELF AT ME, ARMS wide open for a hug. I couldn't help but laugh as I caught her mid-air. Her boundless energy was like a shot of adrenaline straight to the heart.

"You bitch!"

"Well, well, well, if it isn't the werewolf shifter," I teased, giving her a squeeze before setting her back on her feet before my legs gave out. "Miss me much?"

Lily gave me a playful shove. "You have no idea. You disappeared on us, and we thought you'd gone all MIA on the pack."

I chuckled, shaking my head. "No, just something I had to do."

Lily looked me up and down, her dark reddish-brown fur shining in the dappled sunlight. "You look different, you know? Older, wiser, maybe?"

I winked at her. "I've been through some crazy stuff. Let me introduce you to my motley crew." I gestured to Finn and Nia, who had joined us where we stood in the pack courtyard.

Lily's eyes sparkled with curiosity as they landed on our newcomers.

I flashed a grin. "Meet Finn and Nia. They're Fae."

Lily's excitement was palpable. "Fae, huh? I've heard tales, but I've never laid eyes on one. I really thought that was a myth. Pleasure to meet you both."

Nia inclined her head regally. "Likewise. Shifters are creatures we don't have in our realm. I look forward to learning more about your people."

Finn grinned at my pretty friend. "I've heard great things about the Clover pack. Excited to see the mortal realm for myself."

Lily's flirty side was in full swing as she shot Nia a timid smile. I squinted at her for a second. Lily? Timid? I didn't think those words could exist in the same sentence. "We'll have to show you around."

Nia chuckled, her regal facade softening. "I'd appreciate that."

As the introductions rolled on, I turned to Oliver. "And this is

Oliver, our resident halfling. You know him already, but now you can know the real him."

Lily raised an intrigued eyebrow. "A halfling? Like Rowan?"

Oliver nodded, a mix of pride and confidence in his expression. "Yup, that's me. Half-Fae, half-mortal witch, all charm."

Wolfe, the hulking bear-shifter Alpha, approached. "Seems like you've gathered quite the interesting bunch." He pulled me into a hug, and I hugged him back. It was nice to be back in the company of friends.

I smiled, enjoying the moment. "You could definitely say that. We'll probably need your help through this."

Wolfe's knowing gaze met mine as we separated, and I saw him shoot a quick wink at Callan who was glowering off to the side. "You know we'll support you. This was personal the second they started killing shifters."

My confidence soared with the support of my pack. "Thanks, Wolfe. But trust me, it won't be a cakewalk. She's got power and company."

"It's a good thing you came back," he said to me, shooting a pointed look at Callan. "We had no idea what had happened to you both."

Callan frowned. "I left a note."

"'Rowan. Be back later,' is quite literally the worst note I have ever read, Cal. If I knew where you had gone, I would have sent out a search party."

Callan shrugged, looking a tad bit sheepish, but didn't apologize. He wasn't that type of guy, not when he was doing something he thought was right.

"At least I left one."

CHAPTER NINETEEN

My peaceful slumber was shattered by the piercing sound of screams. I bolted upright in bed, heart racing, and didn't need to be a genius to figure out something was terribly wrong. I leaped out of bed, not bothering with clothes, and raced to the pack courtyard.

There, chaos reigned, and I cursed. We'd let ourselves get too comfortable assembling back into pack life. It had only taken one day for them to find us again.

The pack members were struggling to fend off the attackers, but it was clear they were outnumbered and outmatched. I scanned the intruders with a sneer, not surprised to find Cas, Roxy, and a particularly crazed Lexi at the center of the turmoil. How did they even get to this side of the realm? There had to have been another halfling working with them, it was the only way. Oliver was wrong; they couldn't have all been dead.

Cas's eyes locked onto mine, filled with hatred as he looked at me. "That was a clever trick you played on us back there, but you can't keep us out for long. There is not a place in the entire universe that you could go where I won't find you. Give me what's rightfully mine and maybe I'll spare your life."

"I don't have it, you idiot!" I shouted at him, a last-ditch effort to get him to retreat. "I have no idea where it is."

More Fae joined the fray. Each one had hair as vibrant as their elemental magic: fire, water, and earth royals, and they wasted no time diving into the fight. The fire-wielder launched a burst of flames toward my pack members, sending them scrambling for cover. The water manipulator created tendrils of water to ensnare anyone in her path, while the earth-controlling Fae conjured sharp rocks and boulders, creating a treacherous terrain.

I exchanged a look with Callan who had arrived at my side, already in his panther form. His cool Alpha magic coated him, creating an extra magical barrier between him and our foes. The sounds of fighting and clashing rang out around us, but my focus was set on Cas and, drawing on my lightning powers, I charged forward, tired of always being the one to be chased.

The clash between Cas and me was a volatile spectacle of elemental power. We were like two opposing storms, our energies colliding with destructive force. Lightning crackled around us, illuminating the courtyard in blinding flashes.

The arrogant Fae was relentless in his pursuit. He lunged at me with an electrified bolt crackling in his hand, his features contorted with the effort. I darted to the side, narrowly avoiding the deadly strike. The air sizzled where the lightning grazed, leaving a metallic tang in its wake.

I felt the raw power of my newfound abilities coursing through me, a wellspring of energy waiting to be unleashed. I summoned the crackling lightning within me, determined to face my brother head-on.

With a burst of effort, I redirected the incoming bolt, sending it arcing harmlessly into the ground. Cas's eyes widened in surprise, his blonde hair tousled by the electric aura surrounding him. He had underestimated me.

Cas moved with a calculated grace, his eyes alight with raw power. Crackling bolts of lightning danced in his hands as he advanced, launching them toward me with deadly precision. I dodged and weaved, trying to anticipate his attacks, but the sheer force of his magic was overwhelming.

With each clash, I felt my energy wane, my lightning powers flickering like a dying ember. Casimir's relentless assault pushed me back step by step.

Cas's lips curled into a taunting sneer as he cornered me, his electric aura crackling with malevolence. Summoning the last reserves of my energy, I attempted to counter his attack with a surge of lightning. But my powers wavered, and the bolt I released was feeble compared to his. He deftly deflected it, sending it harmlessly into the night sky.

Gasping for breath, I struggled to maintain my footing. Casimir closed in, the gap between us narrowing. "Give it up, little sister," he taunted. "You were never meant to stand against me. If you don't give me what I want, then I will take it. Starting with you."

I was slowly losing this battle, and the weight of that realization pressed down on me. But I couldn't back down, not with my friends relying on me, not with the fate of the Clover pack hanging in the balance. I couldn't let him take me. I'd never see the light of day again. I wouldn't escape him twice.

With one final burst of effort, I mustered the last of my strength and unleashed a surge of lightning toward Cas. He staggered back, his grip on his powers faltering as he tried to avoid my blast.

But before I could seize the advantage, a burst of lightning surrounded him, and he vanished in a smoky residue. He had teleported himself out of harm's way.

"Damn it," I muttered, scanning the chaotic battlefield for any sign of him.

Suddenly, Cas reappeared, but not near me. No, he reappeared behind Wolfe, who was valiantly fighting for his pack and ripping enemies to shreds with his sharp teeth. Cas powered up, releasing a bolt bigger than I'd ever seen from him so far.

Kai, Wolfe's loyal second in command, threw himself in front of the vicious attack aimed at Wolfe's turned back. His limp body hit the ground, and he didn't stir.

An earth-wielding Fae fell, succumbing to the combined power of Finn and Callan. Finn used his air to hold the Fae down, while Callan pounced, making quick work as he ripped out his throat. Cas's voice rang out as he called back to us, his tone filled with venom and triumph at downing one of ours as they ran to an open portal. I looked around for the halfling that would be needed to keep this portal open, but saw no one. "Remember this. You have one week to find the ring. Find it, or I'll come back here, and every member of your precious pack will die."

His ominous words hung in the air, and an intense sense of guilt washed over me. It was my past actions, my decision to hide the ring and erase my memories, that had brought this threat to the Clover pack. The weight of that responsibility pushed in, and I knew I had to find a way to protect my newfound family.

Once the enemy had retreated, Kai's mate, a striking she-dove named Elowen, rushed to his side. Her blood-matted white fur shifted to skin, her body elongating, as she returned to her human form. She let out heart-wrenching sobs as she cradled Kai's lifeless body in her arms, and my heart broke for her.

The sight was gut-wrenching. I watched from a distance, my heart heavy with sorrow and guilt. I had no right to comfort her, given I was the reason he had even been fighting in the first place. All of this was my fault. I needed to distance myself, before anyone else got hurt.

My breathing quickened as my anxiety spiked. I shouldn't have come back to Clover. For everyone's safety.

I wouldn't be here when Cas got back.

Chapter Twenty

Elowen's condition was deteriorating rapidly. I watched her, my heart heavy with sorrow, as she lay on a makeshift bed, her breath shallow and labored. This was my first time witnessing the devastating effects of a broken mate bond, and it was horrifying. The room was filled with an oppressive silence, broken only by Elowen's occasional whimpers of pain. My thoughts drifted to my own life.

Callan was mated to Lexi, the very woman who had orchestrated the attack on us. If he succeeded in killing Lexi, Callan would inevitably follow Elowen into the abyss of death. The pain she must be feeling was unimaginable, and the thought of losing him weighed heavily on my heart as I watched Elowen's struggle.

The cruel reality of mate bonds was no joke. When one half of the bond was lost, the other often followed soon after, wasting away until their soul perished, taking them with it. A heartbreaking fate, and one I wouldn't wish on anyone. And yet, would it be Callan's fate too?

I struggled to find words of comfort or solace with the shifters that trickled in around the clock, but nothing seemed adequate. This was a pain that couldn't be eased with words, and a pain that could have been prevented.

Our pack had gathered in the cabin, faces marked with worry and grief. Wolfe stood at the head of the room, his brow furrowed in thought. Nia, Finn, Oliver, Lily, and the others were scattered around. Nia and Lily stood close together, speaking in low voices as their foreheads almost bumped.

Wolfe cleared his throat, breaking the heavy silence. "We can't change what's happening to Elowen," he began, his voice steady despite the weight of the situation. "I would give anything in the world to be able to help her, to turn back the clock and push Kai out of the way." His voice broke, and he cleared his throat before continuing. "But we can decide what we do next."

He looked around at the faces of his pack, his gaze lingering on me. "Rowan, you've faced these Fae before. Do you have any insights into their tactics or weaknesses?"

I nodded, my mind racing as I recalled our encounters with the Fae. "The Fae are powerful but rely heavily on their elemental magic. The red-haired Fae wields fire, the blue one controls water, and the brown-haired Fae manipulates the earth. We've seen their abilities firsthand, and they're formidable."

Nia raised an eyebrow. "What about you, Rowan? Your lightning magic could be an advantage against them."

I hesitated for a moment before responding. "I'm still learning to control my abilities, but yes." I didn't want to give them false hope, when I knew I'd be leaving before it came to that. I just needed the right moment. And selfishly, I wasn't quite ready to say goodbye.

Finn, who had been relatively quiet until now, spoke up. "You need training, more than just elemental magic. You need to learn how to fight as a group, to anticipate each other's moves, and to use our strengths to our advantage."

Lily chimed in, "And we should seek guidance from the Fae. They have centuries of combat experience. If anyone can help us, it's them."

Wolfe nodded in agreement. "We need to prepare ourselves."

A voice from the back of the room spoke up, its tone dripping with bitterness. "Or we could get rid of the problem altogether. Rowan's presence here has only brought trouble. We should send her away and be done with it."

I turned to see who had spoken, a woman I'd only met in passing. The sentiment hung in the air, and I could feel the eyes of the pack on me, waiting for my response.

Lily, always one to speak her mind, was the first to object. "That's not fair. Rowan's one of us, and she's helped us more than once. We can't just turn our backs on her."

Nia's voice carried authority as she added, "You need our knowledge, and we won't do this without Rowan."

I felt a mix of emotions surging within me. I had found a place among these shifters, a sense of belonging I had never known before. The idea of being cast out, of losing everything I had come to cherish, was a terrifying prospect.

Wolfe stepped forward, his presence commanding attention. "We're a pack, and we make decisions together. Majority rules. All in favor of seeking training and guidance from the Fae and defending our home, raise your hand."

One by one, hands went up around the room, and my heart swelled with a sense of unity. They were choosing to fight together, to face the looming threat head-on. If only I had that same outlook.

Callan stepped forward, his face serious. "There's another matter at hand here too. We need to weaken them, or they'll never stop coming for us. For Rowan."

"How do you suggest we do that?"

"We have to kill Cas," I said quietly. It was something I'd been mulling over on my own, and no matter how I turned it over in my own head, killing Cas was the best way to hit the Queen where it hurt. So far she hadn't made an appearance, letting her son do her dirty work. And without him, we stood that much more of a chance.

Wolfe scanned the room, waiting for someone to object.

When no one did, he nodded grimly, his shaggy hair bouncing with the movement. "Then we do what we must."

The hours passed slowly, each minute feeling like an eternity as we watched Elowen's life slip away. There was a profound sense of helplessness in the room, an unspoken acknowledgment that nothing could be done to change her fate. But there was also an undercurrent of fire. These people had been attacked in their homes, and they wanted revenge.

Elowen's breathing had become even more labored, her once-bright eyes now dulled by pain. I sat by her side, my hand resting gently on her arm, offering whatever comfort I could in those final moments, my guilt at Kai being caught in the crossfire driving my actions. Callan stood nearby, his expression a mix of grief and anger.

I couldn't help but feel a pang of fear for him, for what would happen once Lexi was dealt with. The bond between them, broken as it was, still held a powerful sway over Callan. His desire for revenge burned like a relentless fire, and I worried that it might consume him in the end.

"Rowan. Stop looking at me like that," he whispered, his voice barely audible over Elowen's shallow breaths. "I can't let Lexi go unpunished for what she's done."

I turned to meet his gaze, my heart aching for him. "I understand that, Callan, but don't forget the consequences of revenge. It won't bring them back. It will only kill you too."

He clenched his fists, his jaw set, saying nothing more, in typical Callan fashion.

The room slowly filled with the hushed whispers of pack members offering their condolences and sharing stories of the time they had spent with her. It was a bittersweet tribute to a woman who had touched so many lives.

Elowen's breaths grew shallower and further apart, her once-vibrant spirit gradually fading away. The room was filled with the quiet sobs of pack members, their grief palpable as her life ran out.

Then, with a final, shallow breath, Elowen's chest stilled. The light in her eyes flickered and then went out. She was gone.

A heavy silence settled over the room, broken only by the sound of muffled sobs.

Callan stood there, his gaze fixed on Elowen's lifeless form, a haunted expression on his face. I reached out to him, my fingers brushing against his arm, a silent reminder that he wasn't alone, no matter what decision he decided to make.

But as I looked at him, I couldn't help but wonder what would happen when the time came for him to confront Lexi. The bond between them was a powerful force, and it had the potential to shape his destiny in ways we couldn't predict.

As the pack began to plan for Elowen's farewell, the looming threat of Cas and his forces still hung over us, and Callan's desire for revenge burned brighter than ever. It was a volatile mix of emotions, and tensions were high.

But for now, in this moment of grief and loss, all we could do was say our final goodbyes to Elowen and honor her memory in the best way we knew how.

CHAPTER TWENTY-ONE

The sun hung low in the sky, casting a warm, golden hue over the training grounds of the Clover pack. A sense of anticipation hummed in the air as the pack members gathered, eager to begin their training sessions. I stood at the edge of the clearing, taking in the sight of my fellow shifters and Fae, all with varying degrees of excitement etched on their faces as they practiced. Nia and Oliver were running drills with a group while I got private training from Finn and Callan.

Finn, who had volunteered for the job, stood beside me. His bright eyes sparkled with enthusiasm as he grinned. "Ready for some training, Rowan?"

"You bet." Couldn't have sounded more enthusiastic if I tried.

As Finn began to instruct me on channeling my innate magical abilities, Callan watched from a distance. His gaze never wavered from me, a heavy presence I couldn't help but feel a surge of Alpha dominance as he observed me, even though he wasn't the one training me in this moment. I tried to focus on Finn's guidance as best I could, doing my best to ignore the heat that bloomed in my belly at the thought of the enigmatic rogue. It was as if his very proximity demanded my attention.

Finn patiently guided me through the basics of elemental

magic, teaching me how to connect with the natural energy around me, not only within. I was a quick learner, and with Finn's encouragement, I soon managed to conjure a small, controlled ball of lightning. It was much improved from what I had been able to do so far, which was just throwing out wild blasts as often as I could. They sparked in my palm, flickering with bright bursts of electricity.

Finn clapped his hands in approval. "Well done, Rowan! You're a natural." He almost never stumbled over the name now.

I grinned, a sense of accomplishment washing over me. "Am I really a natural if I'm just re-learning the things I forgot?" I leaned in, giving him a side hug as I let the lightning dissipate, grateful I was catching on to my powers. Not being able to unlock my memories had been devastating, but it was also like it had allowed me to better embrace my powers.

My training session with Finn had been enlightening, to say the least. The Fae had an innate connection to the elemental forces of nature, and Finn was no exception. His deep-blue eyes sparkled with excitement as he explained the basics of elemental magic to me.

After my session with Finn, it was Callan's turn to train me. He was a different kind of teacher, sharp and calculating. He didn't have Finn's gentle demeanor; instead, he pushed me to my limits, determined to make me a formidable shifter. Or as formidable as a bunny could get.

In my bunny form, I hopped nimbly around the training area, using my enhanced senses to detect his movements. Callan, in his panther form, stalked me with deadly precision. He taught me to harness my instincts, enhancing my senses further and sharpening my reflexes. Our training sessions were intense. As we trained, I found myself pushing not only my own limits but his as well, silently challenging him to open up.

Our training was a dance of predator and prey, teacher and student, and as the days passed, I couldn't deny the chemistry that existed between us. But it was a dangerous path to tread.

The week of relentless training unveiled a remarkable transformation within me. Each day, I delved deeper into my unique affinity for lightning under Finn's expert guidance. His azure eyes held a wealth of knowledge, and he patiently led me through the intricacies of manipulating this electric force. We stood amidst nature's beauty, and as I reached out to the elements, lightning responded, surging through me like a river.

Callan's training sessions were demanding. He pushed me to hone my shifter abilities. There was none of Finn's practiced patience and kindness with Callan. The sprawling forest served as our training arena, and soon I learned to channel my speed and agility. He drilled into me, until I could control it with precision, shifting in only a few seconds flat.

THE WEEK OF GRUELING TRAINING LEFT ME FEELING FAR from perfect, but I couldn't deny the leaps and bounds of progress I had made. Confidence surged within me like a tide, and I could feel the lightning coursing through my veins, eager to respond to my commands.

Finally, I was able to get some alone time with Lily. We had barely spent time together since my return, both of us swept up in the hectic rhythm of our lives as she spearheaded several classes for self-defense. A girls' day was long overdue, and we settled into a table at the cafeteria with steaming cups of coffee, ready to catch up.

"You are not allowed to leave me like that ever again," she demanded.

"I'm sorry," I said sheepishly. "But I had to. I needed to try."

"Callan was insufferable while you were gone. I was secretly glad when he dipped out because he was getting on my nerves."

A frown split my brow as I looked at her. She rolled her eyes, tossing her dark curtain of hair over one shoulder. "That boy clearly has it bad for you."

Laughter exploded from me, and I almost choked on my coffee in the process. "He has a mate, Lily. A living, breathing mate that isn't me. I'm sure you're just misunderstanding."

She raised a brow. "Just because he has a mate doesn't mean he can't also be into you."

"What about you?" I threw back at her, eager to get the conversation off me. She didn't know what she was talking about. "You seem to be spending quite a bit of time with Nia." I could be wrong, but I sensed something there, different from the way Lily and I were friends.

She blushed, something I had never seen my friend do before, and I broke into a wide smile. "Oh, I'm totally right, aren't I? You and Nia?"

"Shush! We're just . . . hanging out. Getting to know each other." She looked down at her hands, suddenly withdrawn. "I was worried about telling you. Or anyone. Same-sex couples among shifters are rare. It's counterintuitive to our need for survival. My parents would rip my head off."

I raised an eyebrow, mildly offended. "Lily, I hope you know me better than that. I'm certainly not going to judge you. Who cares who you want to love? If your parents can't accept you for that, then it's their loss."

No child, no matter how old, should have to live in fear of how their parents would react to something as simple as who they chose to love. There were bigger issues in the world, like war and famine and Queens that were hellbent on destroying the universe. Everyone should just mind their own damn business.

Lily sighed in relief, her shoulders relaxing. "Thank you. It's just . . . I'm really into Nia. We've been getting to know each other, and I can't explain it, but I feel this inexplicable connection. Like I can't breathe when she's around, I'm so nervous. It's kind of scaring me, if I'm being honest."

My eyes widened in understanding, and I couldn't help but grin. "That's amazing."

She blinked, surprised. "You don't care?"

I chuckled softly. "I only care that you're happy. And Nia is good people. She's saved my ass more than a few times."

The cafeteria's door swung open, and in walked Finn and Wolfe, deep in conversation as they joked back and forth. When they spotted us, they made their way over, and Finn slapped Wolfe on the back with a laugh.

"Hello ladies, you won't believe the bromance that's been brewing here! Did I use that word right? I just learned it!" Finn exclaimed, his blue eyes twinkling mischievously.

Wolfe chuckled, his unruly brown hair tousled. "We've been bonding over magical defenses and a shared love for the ladies."

"And the *slang*," Finn chimed in, beaming with pride that he'd used another word he had learned.

Lily giggled while I fought the urge to barf. "It's good to see you two getting along so well."

Wolfe nodded, his expression turning more serious. "Speaking of defenses, we've been working hard on preparing the pack for the upcoming fight. Thanks to Finn's expertise, we've implemented some new magical protections."

Finn grinned proudly. "We've got wards! Plus, I've been teaching the pack how to fight against elemental magic in the most effective ways."

I leaned in, intrigued. "Tell us more about these magical defenses."

Wolfe shared a knowing look with Finn before continuing, "One of the enchantments we've set up is an alarm system linked to the pack's territory boundaries. If any hostile forces breach it, we'll be alerted instantly. We've also created cloud barriers that will slow down any intruders and deflect spells, giving pack members precious time to react and defend."

Finn added, "It's going to take a lot for them to get through. We took a quick trip back to the Faerie realm and I picked up some helpful items." He winked conspiratorially at me. He meant his artifact collection. I'd almost forgotten about that.

Lily's eyes widened in appreciation. "That sounds impressive."

Wolfe nodded. "We're doing everything we can to keep the pack safe. We've also been coordinating with the other Fae and Oliver to ensure we have support when the time comes, and from nearby packs."

Despite the encouraging camaraderie and the promising prospects for our pack's defense, I couldn't shake the persistent gnaw of guilt and doubt that had taken root within me. As I sipped my coffee and listened to Finn and Wolfe discuss the magical safeguards, a whirlwind of thoughts swirled through my mind.

Why am I still here? The question reverberated in my head like a relentless echo. In the past, whenever danger had approached, my instincts had driven me to flee, to protect myself by leading threats away. But I hadn't brought myself to leave yet. I was too attached.

The twinge of doubt was only exacerbated when I overheard hushed voices from a nearby table, unaware of my presence.

"I don't understand why she's still here," one of them grumbled. "She's just putting us all in danger. She's not one of us."

His companion nodded in agreement, a twisted snarl on her face. "She's an outsider. This is all her fault in the first place. We were better off before she came here."

Their words cut through me like a knife. *Are they right?* I wondered.

I shifted uncomfortably in my chair, my unease palpable. The bonds of friendship and the sense of responsibility weighed heavily on my shoulders. Part of me longed to slip away in the night, to protect my newfound friends and pack by luring our enemies away, just as I had always done. Yet, I also knew that running away was not a solution. Not for long. Cas would catch me, and I had no idea where the ring was. I'd barely even had time to start looking.

He'd catch me, and then I'd be his prisoner.

Their prisoner.

But what if I could escape? The question gnawed at my conscience, festering like an open wound. I'd learned a lot about my powers. I hadn't had the chance to learn how to make portals yet, but I had great control of my lightning, and I could hide a lot easier from the lumbering Fae if I was in rabbit form.

As I sat there, a dangerous idea began to take shape in my mind. Maybe, just maybe, it was best for everyone if I were to slip away unnoticed before our adversaries returned. I could lead them astray, put distance between them and our pack, and bear the consequences alone.

My heart ached with the thought of leaving behind the friends I'd grown to care for, but darkness whispered insidiously in my ear. It was the only way to ensure their safety. I just had to be fast enough.

THE AIR CRACKLED WITH TENSION AS I APPROACHED Callan for our training session, my mood sour and my resolve waning. The decision I was contemplating weighed heavily on my mind, and every interaction felt like a struggle against the brewing storm within me.

Callan, his emerald-green eyes sharp and observant, wasted no time in acknowledging my state. "You're not yourself today," he remarked, his voice low and laced with concern.

I clenched my fists, frustration bubbling to the surface. "No, I'm not," I replied tersely, my words heavy with the weight of unspoken thoughts.

He suggested a hand-to-hand sparring session, a silent invitation to release some of the pent-up emotions. I nodded, and we began, our movements fluid yet charged with an unspoken tension.

The training grounds stretched before us, bathed in the soft, golden glow of the afternoon sun. Callan and I stood at opposite ends of the makeshift arena, the air heavy with anticipation. It was evident that something was amiss, and it added an extra layer of tension to our sparring session.

As we circled each other, I couldn't help but notice the way Callan's muscles rippled, his bare chest on full display. His rugged, scar-laden torso spoke of battles fought and won. Sunlight kissed his skin, casting a warm, bronze hue over his chiseled features, making him appear even more formidable.

I had opted for a more casual attire, my white tank top clinging to my frame as I moved. My ears twitched with a mix of anxiety and adrenaline, and my hips swayed in tune with my erratic heartbeat as I stayed light on my feet, waiting.

Our initial strikes were cautious, testing each other's reflexes and defenses. Callan's movements were powerful and precise, each punch and kick delivered with a controlled force that left no room for error. I relied on my agility, darting in and out of his reach, attempting to land quick, strategic blows but never did. He was always one step ahead of me when we fought like this. The tension in the air was palpable, and every move we made felt like a subtle dance, a battle of wits and physical prowess.

As we sparred, our bodies gravitated toward each other, and I couldn't deny the electricity that simmered beneath the surface. Callan's scent—a mix of earth and the outdoors—enveloped me, and the heat radiating from his skin was almost intoxicating. The energy between us crackled.

Despite my snarky demeanor, I couldn't escape the truth that had been gnawing at me. Leaving this place, these people, and Callan behind wasn't a decision I could make lightly. I grappled with my inner turmoil as our sparring session intensified, each clash of limbs and exchange of blows mirroring the internal battle I waged within myself.

It was a clash of strengths and vulnerabilities, a silent question and answer.

Our bodies moved in a symphony of combat, our every motion calculated and precise. Callan's eyes bored into mine, his gaze unwavering even as we exchanged blows. The tension between us was palpable, and I knew there was more to our clash than just physical training.

Callan finally broke the silence. "What's going on with you?" His voice was low and gruff, a stark contrast to the controlled violence of our sparring. His words held a note of concern, and his brows furrowed as he studied my face.

I parried one of his strikes, my response laced with sarcasm. "Why, Callan? Can't a girl just enjoy a friendly sparring session without having something be wrong?"

He chuckled, a deep, rumbling sound that sent shivers down my spine. "You can, but not when you're making a face like you're thinking of murdering someone."

I sighed, relenting to the unspoken question in his emerald eyes. I could have lied, but I didn't. I couldn't. "I've been thinking of leaving."

The tension between us seemed to grow, and Callan struck out, managing to get a grip on my wrist. "Leaving?" His voice was softer now, tinged with a hint of something I couldn't quite place.

I nodded, trying to keep my tone light despite the weight of my words. "I've never been one for sticking around anyway. It's better off if I go, isn't it?"

Callan released my wrist, and we stepped back from each other, our chests heaving with exertion. He looked at me with a mixture of understanding and something else, something deeper. "That's the dumbest thing I've ever heard. Just stay and fight."

I sighed, my shoulders slumping. "It's not that simple, Callan. They're coming back for that ring, and I don't have it. I don't even know where to begin looking for it!"

He took a step closer. "We can find it together."

I met his eyes, the unspoken tension between us growing stronger by the second. "You've got your own demons to face. I can't be the reason you risk your life."

His voice was rough as he spoke, a hint of vulnerability breaking through his usual stoic facade. "You're more important than you think, Rowan."

I swallowed hard, my heart pounding in my chest.

"Callan," I whispered, "it's not about importance. It's about me not letting anyone take the fall for me anymore. There's too much pain, too much death already."

He backed away, anger tightening his jaw as he withdrew, and his walls slammed back into place.

Our sparring session continued, the intensity between us not diminishing in the slightest. Callan and I were evenly matched, each move countered with precision. But as the minutes passed, a subtle shift in our rhythm occurred, a silent challenge that had us throwing increasingly harder blows.

It happened in the blink of an eye. A miscalculated step, a deflected strike, and I found myself sprawled on the ground, my back against the earth, with Callan's strong form hovering over me. The air between us thickened, holding me captive.

Neither of us moved, our rapid breaths the only sound in the clearing. The scent of sweat and exertion hung in the air, but there was an underlying current of something else.

Callan's voice was low, his words barely more than a breathless whisper. "You're a fighter, Rowan. You don't give up easily."

I gazed up at him, our faces mere inches apart, our breaths mingling. "And neither do you," I replied, my voice equally hushed, but a challenge all the same.

His gaze met mine, a hint of desire smoldering in his eyes as he said nothing, the hard length of his body pressed against mine. I swallowed hard, my heart pounding in my chest. I knew the boundaries I'd set for myself, the reasons I couldn't give in to this desire, but in that moment, they seemed impossibly distant.

My eyes darted down to his lips, my tongue coming out to wet mine involuntarily as I dragged my gaze back to his.

Callan's lips brushed against mine, a feather-light touch that sent a jolt of electricity through me. It was a test, a question, a silent plea for permission. And as much as I tried to resist, I responded, my lips parting, inviting him in.

Our kiss was like fire and lightning, a clash of passion and longing that had simmered beneath the surface for far too long. In that stolen moment, we forgot the world around us, lost in a world of sensation and desire as our tongues danced, my core heating until I thought I might ignite.

But reality came crashing back all too soon. The sound of a twig snapping nearby jolted us apart, and I scrambled to my feet, my cheeks flushed. Callan rose with a grace that belied his rugged appearance, his eyes still locked on mine.

"We should. . . get back to training," I muttered, my voice shaky.

"Training's over," he said tersely before turning and walking away, leaving me standing there, my heart racing. My heart hammered against my ribcage, and the heat that had coursed through my body still lingered, my limbs weak.

I watched his retreating figure, his broad shoulders and powerful stride creating a cavern of distance in no time.

With a shaky breath, I ran a hand through my disheveled hair, my fingers trembling slightly. I couldn't ignore the tingling sensation on my bruised lips, the lingering memory of his kiss fresh in my mind. Part of me longed to chase after him, to demand answers. But another part, a more cautious and self-protective part, held me back.

It would never end in my favor.

He had a mate.

CHAPTER TWENTY-TWO

The rustic dining hall, lit by the soft flicker of candlelight, enveloped us in a warm, intimate embrace as we sat. The tables groaned under the weight of hearty dishes, the scent of succulent roasts and freshly baked bread enticing our senses. It was our final meal together before the looming day when Cas had said he would return.

I picked at my food, my appetite overshadowed by the heavy burden I carried on my shoulders. My gaze wandered across the table to Callan, who seemed lost in thought, eyes locked onto his plate as if it held the secrets of the universe. We hadn't talked since we'd shared that earth-shattering kiss yesterday.

Beside me, Nia and Lily chatted, their banter a ray of sunshine in the impending storm. They were near attached at the hip.

"Lily, I swear you have the weirdest taste in food. Bacon and maple syrup?" Nia asked.

Lily shrugged with an impish grin, looking through her lashes at Nia. "It's all about that sweet and savory combo. Keeps things interesting. Kind of like us, I hope?" Lily's timidness was adorable, her heart out on her sleeve for all to see. Nia chuckled and shook her head, her amusement evident as a slight blush creeped up her cheeks, but she said nothing.

Callan's lips twitched, the ghost of a smile playing at the corner of his mouth.

We locked eyes for a heartbeat too long, and in that fraction of a second, I glimpsed something dark underneath. The tension that had been simmering between us since our stolen kiss hung like a thick fog, obscuring everything else.

But as quickly as it came, the moment passed. Callan withdrew his gaze, focusing on his plate with renewed intensity, as if he needed the meal to shield himself from me. A sliver of anger blossomed in me. The hot and cold act was infuriating.

Wolfe rose from his seat, casting a long shadow across the room as he stepped into the flickering candlelight. The atmosphere was thick with apprehension as he brought us back to reality. His voice, like the rumble of distant thunder, commanded our attention.

"To my pack and welcome guests," he began, his eyes scanning the faces of those gathered around the rough-hewn wooden table, "tonight, we dine together, but tomorrow, we will be challenged. We will fight."

Tension rippled through the room. The impending confrontation weighed heavily on them all. Wolfe's gaze hardened as he spoke, displaying the power that told them why they called him Alpha.

"Let there be no doubt—we do not possess what they seek. But we also know that they won't simply accept our word. We're in for a battle that will test our strength and unity." His voice held a steely resolve. "Tomorrow, we fight not just for ourselves but for the safety and future of this pack. We fight for our lives."

I listened intently, guilt building inside of me. As Wolfe spoke, my unease only grew. The pack faced an uncertain future, all because I was here.

"If you want to leave, now is the time. I won't force anyone to stay here that doesn't want to be."

Wolfe's speech resonated through the room, casting a somber spell over our gathering as we all looked around, seeing who would leave. The flickering candlelight danced across the faces of the pack as nobody moved.

With each passing moment, the decision to leave tonight grew more solid in my mind. I wouldn't stand up now, but I wouldn't stay here and watch them die.

What would happen to Callan if Lexi died? Their stupid mate bond made everything more complicated. It was undeniable that Callan would suffer immensely if she died. I'd seen firsthand what happened to Elowen, and he seemed hell-bent on repeating that. A knot formed in my chest at the thought of him enduring such pain because of me.

As I watched Nia and Lily bathe in their bliss, I couldn't help but envy the connection they'd formed, a stark contrast to the dark cloud of uncertainty that hovered over me and Callan.

I contemplated my decision in silence before finally making up my mind. I silently said my goodbyes to each face that had become important to me, I memorized each face, searing them into my memory.

This would be the last time I'd see them.

Chapter Twenty-Three

As I moved with trembling hands later that night, I packed my backpack, stark memories flooding through me as I prepared to sneak out like a thief in the night. I recalled the mirthful giggles shared with Lily and Evie, the excitement that had buzzed in the air as we'd prepared for the party in this very cabin. Evie, who had never gotten to go to a party of her own. Evie, who was taken from the world too soon, because of me.

My thoughts drifted to Callan and my memories of him in this place. The Mating Moon had cast a seductive spell upon us, drawing him back to my cabin, where desire had ignited like wildfire. At least for me it had. In the moonlit hours, his lips had explored every inch of me without expecting any in return, and the memory of that passionate night still sent shivers down my spine.

The nostalgic regret threatened to engulf me. Each creak of the wooden floorboards, each gust of wind that rustled the leaves outside, echoed with a poignant history that now stood at a crossroads. My heart ached with the weight of my decision, but I knew that leaving was the only way to protect my newfound family. It wasn't that long ago that I had shown up here, jaded and broken, and they'd welcomed me in. I never did get those ten thousand dollars, but I had new skills now, and I'd find a way to survive.

Running was the one thing I'd always been good at.

The choice was mine, and it was now or never. I kicked my boot against the floorboard, not sure what I was waiting for. *Get your shit together. You never wanted any of this in the first place.* My words to myself did the trick, and I gathered my resolve around me like a shawl as I exited into the cool night air, not giving myself any longer to dwell and change my mind. This was for the good of the pack. I didn't know how he was doing it, but Cas had to have been tracking me. It was too much of a coincidence that he'd found me everywhere we had been. He would know that I was no longer with the pack and follow me, I'd bet my life on it. From there, I'd figure it out.

It was still and quiet outside of my cabin, not even crickets chirping in the surrounding forest in the dead of night. I'd been running over the scenarios since dinner, and I'd come up with a solid plan. Well, as much of a plan as I could come up with running on no sleep. The defenses designed to protect us were just that: defenses. Created to keep intruders out, but they said nothing about keeping us in. I was fairly certain if I went out through the back of the pack lands and not the front, I could make it out with no one seeing me. Maybe it would trip as I left, but by the time they figured out what happened, I'd be long gone. I was trackable, especially if Oliver still had my blood from when I'd given it to him when we first met, but at least I'd be away from the pack. I'd escape first, and then plan later.

I shrunk low to the ground, my simple all-black outfit of jeans and a sweater whispering against my skin as I moved. I skirted around my cabin, my eyes peeled out for anyone, but at this time of night everyone should've been sleeping. My gaze landed on the mansion my cabin was dwarfed by, where Wolfe lived alone as the Alpha of the pack, and a pang of regret went through me. I hoped that one day, when this was all over, I'd be able to make my way back here and reconcile the life I had started to build.

Tears welled in my eyes, and I immediately shut that shit down. I didn't deserve to cry, nor did I have time to. I had to get the fuck out of here before anyone saw me. I continued my cautious pace, taking my first step into the dense forest, the darkness pressing in like an old friend.

Using my new shifter prowess, I enhanced my senses as Callan had taught me, my eyes sharpening enough that I could make my way through the dark. My other senses came alive, the damp scent of the forest permeating my nose, while my ears twitched at every snap of the leaves underneath my feet. If I had a way to carry my stuff, my bunny form would have been much more efficient, but I had to work with what I could.

I progressed through the forest, making quick work of my path, the cabin far behind me now, just a small shape in the receding distance as I advanced. With my normal eyes, I wouldn't have been able to make out anything in the darkness. Ahead of me, I began to make out the edge of the magical wards thanks to my Faerie magic, having put at least a mile between me and my cabin.

As I approached the barrier, the shimmer of magic glowed beneath the moonlight, an all-encompassing protection that extended far above my head. I paused, taking a deep breath as I prepared to step across the barrier, testing my theory once and for all. If a big siren sounded, then I would bolt.

My nerves faded out with my exhale and I stepped forward, ready to embark on the next chapter, until a loud snap sounded behind me and I whirled, pivoting to see Callan standing behind me. *How had I let him sneak up on me so easily?* His eyes bored into mine, rage stiffening his jaw as he glared at me.

He was *pissed.*

"Go back to your cabin. *Now.*" Callan's voice was sharp, like little needles pricking my skin with the weight of my betrayal. His accent made its appearance, deepening with emotion. "This is reckless, don't you see that? You're putting yourself and the pack in danger."

I struggled to maintain my composure. "The pack is already in danger, Callan! He's too powerful. He's tracking me, you know he is. If I leave, he'll follow me, and then the rest of the pack will be safe. No one else has to get hurt."

Callan closed the distance between us, his hand gripping my arm firmly. I should have backed away, should have shaken his hold, but I was entranced, and I hated myself for it. I never wanted to let someone have this kind of pull over me, and yet here I was. Melting into a puddle for a man who already had a mate. My entire body was a ball of heat, with the spot his hand touched blazing the brightest. "As much as you constantly try to do the opposite, I won't let you get yourself killed."

My resolve wavered as I met his eyes, that same connection that always burned between us ever-present. Part of me wanted to go along with it, let him drag me back to my cabin, where I felt safe and protected. But then I thought of Evie, of Kai and Elowen. All the teens Lexi had slaughtered for the spell that freed the Queen. The spell I had cast.

I couldn't let even more people die for me. Because of me.

The moonlight bathed us in its silvery glow, casting long shadows that seemed to dance around us. I looked up at the moon, a stark reminder of the connection we had shared during the Mating Moon, before turning back to him. Our faces were mere inches apart, his grip on my arm holding firm.

"How can you place so much regard on my life, but not on yours?" I lashed out at him, my anger and resentment in his choices brimming to the surface. "If this fight happens, you'll kill Lexi, and then you'll die. Or better yet, you'll change your mind and decide you really do love her." It slipped out before I meant it to, my immaturity rearing its ugly head. I didn't want that to be the case. I should have been worried about his life, not his heart. It would be a lie to say that I was only running for the good of the pack. Mate bonds were strong, and I wanted to be a little selfish. I saw the way Elowen had wasted away after Kai died. That kind of pain and despair was real, I believed in it now.

Mate bonds were real. And Callan had one, with Lexi. I was scared shitless of both outcomes. Either Callan loved somebody else, or he died. I didn't see an in-between. Only heartbreak for me, either way. I was already too far gone to protect myself anymore.

I'd fallen for Callan without even realizing it.

"You are so goddamn frustrating," he snapped. His hands slid to my waist as he forced me a few steps back, until my back thudded against a thick forest tree. Before I could speak, he crushed his lips to mine, catching me completely off guard. His kiss was dominant, unrelenting, as our tongues tangled together, entwining in a fierce battle of wills. Even while kissing we were at odds with each other, warring for who was the most stubborn. Who would be right. It was always like that with us. He pressed into me, my body burning under his touch as he blazed a trail with his fingertips. When I thought I might have forgotten how to breathe, he pulled away, giving me only a small amount of space.

Callan's gaze bored into mine as he tilted my chin up to look at him, speaking slowly so I couldn't miss a single word. "I. Do. Not. Love. Lexi. And I know now that I never really did. I can't explain it, because I know that's not the way it's supposed to work, but it's true. I don't love her, and I never will."

He dipped his head down, his teeth firmly nipping my swollen lips, which he then covered with a soft kiss. Pain mixed with pleasure and I almost moaned, but managed to hold it in, just barely. His words registered in my head, my heart still pounding in my ears.

"I'm tired of fighting this," he told me softly as his kisses moved to feather my jawline, coming to a rest near my ear. His hot breath sent goosebumps rippling over my skin, and my hands came up to fist in his shirt. I wasn't sure if I was trying to push him away or pull him closer, but he made the decision for me.

"Ever since I first saw you, you've been a thorn in my side." He worked the sensitive spot on the side of my neck, and by the time he'd circled back to my ear, I was a quivering mess. I should have pushed him away, but I couldn't. I didn't want to.

He drew back, his smoldering eyes leaving me breathless. "So headstrong, challenging me at every turn. Sometimes talking to you made me want to punch a wall. And yet, I couldn't get you out of my head. I still can't. I built up every wall, and somehow you still managed to barge your way in. Stubborn little idiot." He kissed me again, somehow even more intense than the first, his hot mouth devouring mine as I threw myself into it. His hands slid from my waist, gently caressing my curves until they ended buried in my hair, and this time I moaned, my body pushing forward with need.

When we finally came up for air, he rested his forehead against mine, his body never moving away from mine. "What have you done to me, Rowan?"

"You have a mate." My voice finally decided to work, blurting out the first thing I could think of, and my biggest protest to taking anything further with Callan. I wanted him, more than I'd ever wanted anyone before, but I was also hyper-aware that in this situation, I was the most vulnerable.

"I don't love her." He kissed me again, and I felt my resistance waver, hovering on the edge of a choice that I could never take back. He'd told me his feelings, exactly what I wanted to hear. But I couldn't lose myself in this, not yet.

"You might die tomorrow. Everyone might die tomorrow. I should go."

"I don't care." His hands fell back to my waist, inching their way under the hem of my shirt, electricity sparking across my skin as his strong hands gripped me.

"I have a mate out there somewhere too." He flinched but didn't release his hold on me as my words cut him. I wasn't trying to hurt him, but that was the reality of our situation. He had a mate, and I would too, one day.

"I know," he said finally, as he lifted his head, a vulnerability that I'd never seen shining through. My breath hitched as I glimpsed more into his soul than I ever had before, an unspoken conversation flowing between us as we stared at each other. He knew this would end in him getting hurt, and he didn't care.

"I've tried so hard to resist this. You're in my dreams, you're in my thoughts. Your fucking smell—I smell you the second I walk into a room. You're fucking irresistible. It took everything I had not to pin you to the ground and fuck the shit out of you during training. And don't even get me started on that night during the Mating Moon."

"I'm scared you're going to die," I whispered, my feelings bubbling to the surface as my voice cracked. He was echoing everything I'd been feeling for weeks, but what was the point if he was going to kill Lexi in the morning?

He removed his hands to cup my face, and even if I wanted to look away, I couldn't. "I can handle myself. I'm not dying anytime soon."

"But—"

"I want *you*, Rowan. More than I even want to breathe. If that means one day you're going to trample all over my heart when you find your mate, then so be it. I can take it."

The truth in his words held strong as he looked into my soul, and I felt the rest of my walls shatter into a million pieces as someone finally picked me for the first time.

Chapter Twenty-Four

This time I kissed him, stepping on my tip toes to reach his mouth, all the emotions I had been harboring inside spilling out. It started slow, until I nipped his bottom lip and he let out a low growl, his chest rumbling under my hands as I explored. He pushed me against the tree harder, nudging his knee between my legs, pressing up against my molten core, and I moaned into his mouth at the contact. It wasn't enough. I needed *more*.

I yanked his shirt up and over his head with little resistance, my hands hungrily running across his bare torso. I'd seen him shirtless more than a few times, but this was different, and I relished every moment I got to touch him.

"Fair is fair," he murmured as his hands roamed my body, making quick work of my shirt, throwing it into a crumpled heap on the forest floor. He deftly unhooked my bra with one hand, while the other worked on unbuttoning my jeans. I'd never hated being a girl more than I did in this moment. *Why do we wear so many clothes?*

The forest was silent around us, the darkness enveloping us like its own dirty little secret as we fell into our passion. Finally freed from my jeans, I tried to fumble with his, but his hands gripped my wrists in an iron hold as he yanked them above my head, pinning them with one hand to the tree as he put his knee back between my legs. "Not yet. I am going to do everything I wanted to do to you that night."

His free hand came up to grip my breast, and I arched against his hold, only increasing the pressure of his knee. He dipped his head, taking a nipple expertly into his mouth.

"Callan," I moaned, bucking my hips against his knee shamelessly as he continued his torturous exploration of my body. My wetness was slick against his thigh, my underwear completely soaked through. "Please." I was begging, and I gave zero fucks. I needed more, needed him inside of me *now*.

He chuckled against my breast. "Patience has never been your strong suit. Let me teach you."

He let go of his hold on my wrist and I thought I'd finally get my wish, but instead his mouth descended back onto mine. I lost myself in the kiss, whimpering as his hands explored my breasts, then down towards my aching center but never quite making the contact I yearned for. Frustration built in me as he stoked the flames inside me, building up to a crescendo that couldn't quite spill over.

"Callan!" It came out more of a yell than I meant it to, and I felt his devilish grin against my neck as I was pretty sure he made a hickey. I used to hate it when my piece of shit ex left me hickeys, but with Callan, I couldn't care less. It was a mark of ownership, and I wanted to be his.

He made a torturous trail down my chest, pausing briefly in places that made me absolutely squirm with need under his attention. He dipped until he was eye level with where I wanted him most, and I almost wept with relief when he slid my underwear down my hips. Strong hands gripped my leg, and I squeaked as he lifted it over his shoulder, leaving me completely open, the chill night air doing nothing to appease the fire. My back pressed into the tree for support.

"You have no idea how long I've been wanting to do this

again," was all he said before he dove straight in, his tongue expertly circling my clit as I moaned. It wasn't long before I was on the edge, writhing against his face as he worked me closer and closer to climax. Just as I was about to explode, he pulled away, gently setting my leg down and rising to his full height.

"Are you fucking kidding me?" I complained, a horny rage I'd never felt before exploding inside me. His hand shot out, quick as a snake as he wrapped it around my throat, squeezing with just the right amount of pressure as he brought his face to mine, pushing me into the tree as he controlled my breathing.

"Patience. The next time you get to come, it'll be around my cock." That shut me right up, and the self-satisfied smirk that toyed at the corner of his mouth made me want to simultaneously smack him and ride his face into oblivion.

Men.

I wasn't one to be outdone. I gasped, pretending he was squeezing too tight, and his eyes widened as he loosened his grip. Taking advantage of the distraction, I gripped his hips and pivoted until his back smacked against the tree, the shock palpable on his face. "What are you doing?" he demanded, but he didn't stop me, and I knew he was strong enough that he could have.

"Patience." I threw his words back at him, my hands already sliding his jeans and underwear down. I dropped to my knees as his rock-solid cock sprang forward, pausing briefly as I took it in. I'd seen it a few times given our shifter nature, but this up close and personal, it was *big* and I questioned if it would even fit.

But I was not a quitter.

I took the head into my mouth, swirling my tongue expertly before taking his hard length as far into my throat as I could. He relaxed into the tree, his eyes watching my every move as I bobbed and sucked. His hands came to tangle in my hair, the soft pants he was letting out driving me wild, spurring my enthusiasm as I sucked him off.

Just when it seemed like he was getting close, I reached a hand up, gripping his balls with a firm pressure as I relaxed my throat,

SAVANNAH LEE

taking him even further than I thought I'd be able to. He let out a loud groan as I tightened my grip with my hand, my tongue teasing around his cock as I deepthroated him. I squirmed, squeezing my legs together with my arousal.

"Don't stop, don't stop," he urged me as he threw his head back, lost in the pleasure I was giving him. His hips surged forward, hands gripping tightly in my hair, and I knew he was close. With a satisfying pop, I let him fall from my lips as I stood back up, his hands sliding from my blonde tresses as he growled in frustration.

He grabbed me, whirling me back around until my back was against the tree, both of us fully exposed in our nakedness beneath the moonlight. His emerald eyes were hooded, clouded with lust as he drank me in.

"I was going to be gentle with you, but not anymore," he said, his hands coming behind me to grip my ass as he hauled me up with ease. I had no choice but to wrap my legs around him, my arms circling his neck as he slammed me back against the tree, the bark biting into my skin as he lined up to my entrance. A sudden thought struck me.

"Wait, don't we need protection?"

He paused. "We aren't mates," he said, and pain ripped through my chest as I remembered. Fertility didn't work for shifters until they'd met their mate. I shut my eyes against it. *Stay in the moment.* My arms tightened around his neck, pulling him in for a long kiss that had me writhing against him.

"Please," I whispered in his ear, giving the lobe a gentle bite.

"Fuck," he groaned, pushing against me with a renewed sense of urgency. He teased the head inside, and I moaned, biting my lip as I stretched to accommodate.

He pushed in further, and even though he'd said he wasn't going to be gentle, I could tell he was trying not to hurt me. "Fuck, you're tight," he groaned as he pushed in further. He froze. "This isn't your—"

I laughed, wiggling my hips to try to hurry him up. "Of course not. There's been a few in here before you."

"Don't mention other men when I'm fucking you," he growled, low in his throat, his hips bucking as he surged into me, his cock burying deep inside. There was a slight burn as I adjusted, but I was so wet that within seconds I was ready, the walls of my pussy squeezing around him as he started to move.

"Oh, fuck!" I moaned as he pulled almost all the way out, before slamming back into me, gliding right over my G-spot. He picked up a rhythm, spurred on by my increasingly desperate moans as my orgasm built. With each thrust the tree dug into my skin, but the pain only heightened my pleasure. I tightened my arms around his neck, rolling my hips to match each of his thrusts as he drilled into me.

Callan kissed me again, and I whimpered into his mouth as his tongue danced with mine, rocketing me over the edge. I broke apart at the seam as I rode my climax out, his pace never letting up. If anything, he fucked me harder, leaves falling from the tree as his relentless strokes rocked us. He leaned into me, shifting his weight so he was able to support me with one hand as I clung to him weakly, aftershocks of my orgasm still coursing through me with each thrust.

His free hand slid between us, finding my swollen clit, and I groaned as he worked the sensitive ball of nerves in time with his thrusts. "Callan," I panted, gasping as I fought to keep myself together, threatening to break apart completely as he built me up again. "I can't."

"Yes, you can," he commanded. He rammed into me even harder, swiveling his hips in just a way that he hit all my most sensitive parts, his fingers still circling my clit in a relentless attack on my sanity. "Come for me."

That was all it took, and I came again, screaming in the midnight forest. I dug my fingernails into his back as I came, clawing at him in a pleasure-crazed frenzy. I'd had sex before, but no one had ever fucked me like that. He moved faster, harder, as he approached his own climax, and I clenched, tightening my pussy around him as hard as I could, eliciting the sexiest moan I'd ever heard as I did.

"You smell so fucking good," he told me, burying his face in my neck as he thrust, and I knew he was getting close. I reached my head to the side, sinking my teeth into his shoulder, harder than I probably should have, and he groaned.

"You're going to be the death of me," he said, before dipping his head back towards my neck, giving me a matching bite. He built me up for a third time that I didn't think I could survive as his movements got more and more urgent. I tightened my pussy again, and he let out a guttural shout as he swelled inside me, both of us launched over the edge as he came.

"Mine," he growled into my neck, as he let me slowly slide down his body and back on my own two feet. He didn't let go, pulling me into his embrace, tightly, as if I might fly away.

"Yours," I agreed, not knowing how much longer I would be able to say that.

CHAPTER TWENTY-FIVE

"**R**owan."

I stirred, stretching languidly as I slowly opened my eyes. The memories of the night before trickled back to me, my heart swelling. I was the good kind of sore, the kind that only comes about after a night of getting thoroughly fucked, and I smiled to myself. We'd gone most of the night, until we were both so exhausted we had to sleep, the next day looming over our heads like a guillotine. I looked around for Callan, but only the bag I had packed and my dagger lay on the ground nearby. A pit of dread settled in my stomach.

"Callan?" I called softly, the early morning light casting a glow around the forest that I would have stopped to admire if I wasn't on the verge of panicking. I sharpened my hearing, cocking my head as I listened intently, but there was nothing. Did he change his mind and decide he didn't want to do this with me? Had I misunderstood, and this was just a one-time thing? Doubts raged through my head as I slowly stood, making sure to loop my dagger back into the sheath I had clipped to my jeans. I wasn't planning on stabbing him, unless he really did leave me in the forest all alone, but you never knew.

"*Rowan.*"

With my enhanced shifter hearing, I picked it up that time. It sounded like Callan, but his words sounded garbled, distorted somehow. I looked back toward my cabin, but the world was quiet, only the slight beginnings of the pack starting to wake up to prepare for the day.

"Over here."

I whipped my head to the right, focusing on the shimmering magical barrier of the wards. It was a darker color than I remembered, but visibility had been pretty bad the night before. I could barely make out the shape of Callan standing on the other side, the pixels obscuring my vision of the other side. I knew it was hard to see through, given I could see the magic, but I didn't realize it distorted sound too.

"What are you doing?" I called out to him as I approached the barrier.

"Come here," he said, his voice demanding as his silhouette motioned me forward. It was like I could tell his body was there, but the golden magic blocked out all the details of him, so he was just a Callan-sized shadow. Irritation blossomed at his tone. Just because we'd had sex didn't mean he just got to boss me around. "Please," he added.

I'd chosen to stay. I had to make sure the plan we'd worked up was carried out or this was all for nothing. If we killed Cas, then the Queen would be left weakened. Vulnerable. We'd have the upper hand in her stupid game. I just hope I didn't come to regret it.

I stepped up to the magical barrier, eyeing it. I didn't think it would hurt me, but I couldn't see clearly what was on the other side. But if Callan had walked through, then I should be fine. I doubt he would have let me walk through something that was going to hurt me.

I stepped forward, feeling only the barest of a sensation as I walked through, nothing more than a slight shiver of energy, but my stomach dropped when I saw who was on the other side.

"Cas," I said flatly, my hand already pulling my dagger out of its sheath, bearing it protectively in front of me. Of course, it'd been a trap. *You idiot.*

My half-brother glared at me, electricity crackling in his eyes. He had an air of power and danger around him, and he looked more disheveled than I'd ever seen him, his face already hollowed in just one short week. "You look terrible." I spoke more bravely than I felt as I scanned the clearing I'd stepped into.

Cas took a step closer, and I stepped back, my back bouncing against the now solid magical barrier. *Uh-oh.* Behind Cas, two figures stepped forward, and I immediately understood why I couldn't get back through. Roxy's hands swirled with magic as she cast a spell on the barrier behind me, turning it a milky white color. Two other women stood on each side of her with glowing hands, and Lexi's scarred face and fiery mane made her look wild. She grinned at me, her nose twitching as she scented the air. She looked back at me, her eyes narrowed as she bared her teeth. Behind them were even more Fae I didn't recognize and a whole den of venomous naga behind them.

Oh my god, I was going to die.

I didn't give Cas time to give me his supervillain speech. I was sure there was one, there always was with assholes like him, but I wasn't going to stick around and find out. My best weapon against him was the element of surprise. Last time we'd fought head to head, he'd almost had me. Lightning flowed to my fingertips eagerly as I called on it, brimming just under the surface as it waited for my command. Energy thrummed through me as I felt the edges of my hair start to stand up.

"Give me the ring, Olette," he demanded, just as I flung my arms out, hitting him straight in the chest, launching him off his feet. I threw my next burst at Roxy, who tried to dodge, but I clipped her in the shoulder and she was launched to the side with the force of the blast. I sighed in relief as the magic barrier resumed its normal color, still intact and no longer under Roxy's spell. My eyes narrowed on a figure on the other side, slowly pushing himself off the ground with a dazed look on his face. *Callan*. They must have spelled him.

Lexi didn't wait, hunched over and already contorting as she shifted to her wolf form. I was way ahead of her.

One of the many things I'd practiced with Callan was shifting, over and over again until I could do it at the drop of a hat. My bunny was small, which meant I could complete the transformation a lot faster than most larger shifters could, and I used this to my advantage, finishing my shift before she was halfway done.

I didn't dare run back to the pack. Not when I knew Cas was after me. If they could manipulate the barrier, I had no doubt they could find a way through it, and I didn't want to give them any reason to get any closer to the vulnerable pack. And Callan, who I hoped was okay and was getting help. I was so stupid to think I could do this alone.

Without waiting to find out, I bolted through the trees. a snap of a twig tipping me off that Lexi had given chase. I listened hard as I ran, but only heard one pursuer, Lexi's much larger form rustling through the plant life. Shit, they must have stayed by the pack.

A roar ripped through the air and my heart froze. That was a roar I'd recognize anywhere, filled with anger and the promise of death. Callan. Hopefully that was loud enough for the pack to rouse and get on the attack. I didn't know how long that barrier would hold if they were trying to get in.

I spurred my tiny legs on, leaning into my enhanced shifter speed, but I knew I wouldn't be able to outrun a full-grown wolf. My brain, on the other hand, was surely much larger than hers and I would use that to my advantage. My tail swished as I deftly bobbed and weaved between the trees, trying to create the most erratic pattern for Lexi to try to follow. My little legs strained as I ran under logs and through bushes, places I knew she couldn't follow. The only way she would get me to stop was if she hit me, and she'd have to get close to do so.

A resounding growl echoed behind me as she expressed her

frustrations at not being able to catch me. She was surprisingly limber for a large animal, and while she couldn't catch up to me, I was also having a hard time losing her. Still, I kept running, my heart racing as I tried to stay as surefooted as possible. One small mistake would be the difference between life and death. Cas needed information from me, but I wouldn't be so naïve as to think Lexi shared the same sentiment.

Just as I thought I might be gaining a lead, one of my feet got caught on a branch, and I went hurtling forward. In my panic, I rotated my body as best I could before I hit the ground, calling my human form to the surface. I spurred the change on as fast as I could, and my limbs protested in pain as I shapeshifted for the second time in only a short time, but I had no choice. Staying in my bunny form would be a death sentence if she could get her teeth in me. I skidded to a stop on the sharp leaves in my birthday suit, my arms coming up to cover my face as Lexi leaped forward, her claws outstretched menacingly.

Lightning raced from my fingers up my arms as her claws sunk into my flesh. I cried out when they hit bone but kept my grip on my lightning, screaming with pain and effort as I intensified them, pouring more and more of my energy into my arms. Lexi whined, her body seizing as the electricity shot into her, her eyes rolling into the back of her head. I cut the power, her body slumping limply on top of me. I breathed a sigh of relief when I saw her still breathing. *What happens to Callan if I kill Lexi?*

My teeth clenched as I dumped her off to the side, her claws pulling away from my arms with a sickening squelch. I looked down, averting my gaze when I saw bone peeking through the open wounds. I hesitated as I looked over Lexi's prone form, her reddish fur stained with the fresh forest earth. I could kill her, now would be the time, but I knew I couldn't do it. I couldn't risk it.

It didn't seem like anyone had followed us, but the sounds of shouting and fighting drifted toward me through the air, my gut wrenching as I thought of what might be happening to the pack.

We had some fighters, but the Clover pack was small, even with the reinforcements. But they'd shown up earlier than we'd expected, and shifters were a lot more fragile than magic-wielding Fae.

Everything was falling apart.

I wasted no more time, Lexi forgotten as I raced my way back toward the sound of fighting, needing to help my friends. Cas hadn't followed us out into the woods, which meant he was probably back there, wreaking havoc on the pack. I had hoped he'd eventually follow me, let me lead them away from the pack, but that was naïve. By the time I made it, the fight had moved back, more toward the pack lands, which meant the barrier had fallen. *Shit.*

I searched around the ground, quickly locating my clothes and dagger, hurrying back into them. It wasn't as good as armor, but it was better than running into a fight not only covered in blood, but also stark naked. I'd shifted too many times in quick succession, exhaustion already pulling at my tired limbs, begging me to lay down and take a nap. *Not yet.*

I skulked my way towards the sound of battle, hoping to stay undetected. Cas, with his crackling lightning powers, was going toe to toe with Callan, who dodged and weaved between lightning bursts in his panther form, trying his best to get a swipe or a bite in when Cas left himself open, which was almost never. Callan was adept on his feet, but he was murderous in his animal form. He'd learned quickly not to get too close to me if he wasn't sure he would hit. Getting shocked by lightning repeatedly was not a pleasant experience. I sighed in relief that he seemed to be holding his own for now.

The battlefield was pure chaos as the pack battled for their lives under my half-brother's unrelenting army. Roxy, her dark hair flying around her like an ominous storm, threw frightening black clouds of dark magic at Oliver, who adeptly countered with his own fire magic, signs of exertion on both of their faces.

My eyes were drawn to the shifters, the most vulnerable of

anyone on the battlefield. The pack had learned a lot during the week to prepare for the fight, but not all of them were as swift and agile as Callan's panther, and it showed in their fights. Two witches hurled curses and hexes at a group of them, dark tendrils of energy lashing out toward the pack where Wolfe stood at the forefront, huge and menacing in his bear form. He was too big and slow to dodge and weave, so he chose brute force instead, barreling into the nearest witch who shot a dark blast of power that knocked him back.

I gasped as Caleb, a young lynx shifter I'd come to like in training, was blasted by a dark green spell, landing with a thud on the ground, unmoving. It was exactly what I had feared: people getting hurt because of me.

Pure, unbridled rage rose in me as I gripped my dagger tighter, running into the fray to help like an avenging angel at the witch who had cast the spell. A smirk blossomed across her face as she realized who I was, and blackness started pouring from her hands, a dark mist spreading across the ground rapidly toward me.

I couldn't rush her with the mist, so instead I lashed out, using as much energy as I was willing to spare to launch a lightning bolt at her, hitting her right in the chest. She convulsed, the magic cutting off from her hands as she fell over, but the mist didn't retreat like I'd expected it to. It had reached me, and quicker than I could imagine, it wrapped itself around my ankles as it slowly tried to climb me. My skin burned where it touched through my clothes, and I screamed, trying to kick it off. The wind increased suddenly, racing around me in a mini-tornado, and the pain eased as the mist was sucked up. The funnel moved quickly, rising high into the air, a swirling mass of darkness and despair.

"These witches are nasty," Finn told me as he waved a hand, the air he had summoned to save me engulfing the mist, getting smaller and smaller until it ceased to exist, the dark spell completely absorbed. "You can't let them get too close to you. Remember your training." That was all he said before he launched back into battle, throwing an air gust straight into a naga who was advancing on us with his poisoned blade held high.

A wolf shifter near me fell, the water magic of an elemental Fae slicing his throat wide open with the sword he carried on his back as he had the shifter's face encircled in a sphere of water, unable to breathe. I made a move toward them, but it was unnecessary as Lily's brown wolf leaped through the air, landing on the water Fae with a terrifying snarl as she went straight for his throat, tearing it out in one savage bite.

He crumpled to the ground and Lily raised her head to look at me, blood dripping from her mouth as she gave me a grin. On an animal, it looked completely unhinged. My normally sweet friend seemed to be having the time of her life.

Maybe shifters were more capable than I had originally thought.

CHAPTER TWENTY-SIX

I regrouped toward Oliver, who seemed to be struggling to fend Roxy off, her dark magic slowly ticking away against Oliver. She was a formidable opponent, much more so than her counterparts, and I slid right in, throwing my fair share of lightning strikes at her as she skirted us both. Finally, one of Oliver's fireballs connected with an unguarded hip, and she cried out, pushing backward.

"We have to find their halfling," Oliver gritted out as he repelled a particularly nasty shot she sent out in retaliation. There was no doubt about it; she was here to kill.

"What?"

"If we want to trap Cas, we need to gain the upper hand and block his escape point. We're holding our own, but we need to weaken them."

"Go find them," Nia said to Oliver, sliding in seamlessly and adding her blasts. I hadn't seen her during the battle, but she'd clearly been fighting, her armor stained with blood. I'd never been more grateful in that moment that she slept with her armor on, and annoyed at myself for not doing the same thing. She said something softly to him that I couldn't hear over the sounds of battle, and his wide eyes fixed on her before he nodded, disengaging and running off toward the north end of the forest.

Roxy, seeing his escape, tried to blast a spell at his retreating back, but Nia slid into its path, easily parrying it as she threw a water-whip at Roxy, following up with a slash from the katana she wielded. Roxy's eyes widened, not expecting Nia to try to close the distance between them so aggressively, her movements becoming increasingly more frantic as we pressed in on them, a tall shimmering shield blossoming before her. Nia danced around her, taking shots at every opening she could find. I jumped in with bursts of lightning, relentless as we both wore her down until we were all panting and sweaty and Roxy's shield started to waver with her exertion. Roxy threw out a desperate hand, her shield blasting forward and knocking us off our feet as she clapped her hands, and then she was gone.

"What a coward," Nia scoffed as we took a moment to catch our breath, keeping a watchful eye on the battle around us. "It should be an honor to die on the battlefield, like a true warrior."

"If you die, I think Lily might bring you back just to kill you again," I told her. A smirk was her only answer as she spotted a younger raven shifter in trouble. She was doing her best to scratch out the eyes of the Fae she was fighting, but it was a losing battle as the air Fae kept blasting her off course with gusts of wind. Lily pulled up alongside us, her eyes alight as if she was having the most fun she'd ever had. Her free spirit thrived in chaos, and Nia gave her an appraising glance as they made an unspoken agreement, breaking into a run toward the raven shifter in trouble.

A sharp yelp of pain turned my head, my heart wrenching in my chest as I saw Callan thrown back, his fall broken only by the giant oak he slammed into, slumping into a heap with a whimper as he landed. Cas advanced toward him, lightning writhing around his hands, pure deadly energy.

No!

I threw a blast toward Cas, catching him off guard as he made his way toward my panther shifter. The blast hit him in the side, and he sidestepped with a grunt of pain but otherwise stayed standing. The more energy I expended, the weaker I got, and my attacks were dwindling with every blast. There had to be another way to overpower Cas and hope that Oliver made it back in time to help me kill the bastard.

I repositioned as Cas recovered, my body standing directly between him and Callan, the fury on Cas's face making him look even uglier than his personality already did. He narrowed his eyes at me, his eyes zeroing in on a spot on my neck before throwing his head back and laughing. "Oh, dear sister, shacking up with the savages? I'm not even the least bit surprised. You are one of them after all."

My fingers trembled as I threw another attack at him, which he easily deflected as he built up one of his own. I barely managed to dodge out of the way, and I risked a glance over my shoulder, relieved when I saw Callan pushing himself up from the ground, eyes blazing with fury. Cas shot another blast at me, which I barely dodged and responded with one of my own. Callan brushed up against me, his midnight power flooding into me, and I felt part of my strength return before he ran forward. If he was injured from his earlier fight with Cas, he didn't let it show, his lean feline muscles rippling with power as he ran at Cas. I joined him, using the renewed energy he'd given me to take my own shots at Cas.

Cas's eyes widened as we worked in tandem. If I wasn't shooting golden sparks at him, then Callan was right there, slashing and biting at Cas as he tried to circle around him, tried to get him to turn his back against one of us. But he was smarter than that. He kept us at bay on two sides, but I could see the strain his power was causing him, the way his eyes crinkled at the corners, the slight tremor in his hands as he continued to weave blast after blast. I managed to get particularly close to him, my dagger making a deep cut in his thigh. He threw a hand to the sky, and just like that, he was gone in a burst of lightning.

"Goddammit," I ground out, looking around the battlefield for where he could have gone and not seeing him anywhere.

Interrupting my confusion, a screech sounded overhead, and we all looked up to see our new arrivals.

'Hello, little one,' Aura said in my mind as she dove into the fray, easily spearing a naga with her ferocious talons, her muscles tensing as she literally ripped him in half, his blood and guts spilling everywhere.

I was grateful to see Aura again, but it was her companion that shocked me even more. Varus said nothing as he descended, his muscles bulging as he speared a naga of his own, making quick work of the snake-like creature and moving on to the next like a killing machine. I thought I may never see him again, after he'd abandoned us with the shadow beasts. Where was Lithia?

My attention was pulled away from the much-needed reinforcements as Oliver came running back toward us, blood splattered across his face, dying his silver hair a dark maroon. "Where did he go?" He meant Cas, who I had let get away like an idiot. The battle around us was dying out, thankfully in our favor, and Callan moved to wrap around my legs, his body pressed flush against mine as he stayed alert. I reached down, threading my fingers through the soft patch of fur on his back, taking comfort from his presence as I scanned the battlefield for Cas, who was nowhere to be seen. *Coward.*

"He disappeared in a bolt of fucking lightning," I grumbled. I'd made a lot of progress with my powers, but I had no idea how Cas was able to just teleport himself out of danger.

'We can't let him get away,' Callan said into my mind from where we touched.

"We need to find him," I said out loud as I scanned the mayhem, the battle starting to shift in our favor. The elemental Fae were harder to fight, but Nia jumped on Aura's back, casting her water magic while Aura attacked with her feet, a deadly duo as they took on a fire-wielding Fae. "I'm the one he wants. I didn't cut him deep enough to cause serious damage. He's not done with this fight yet." Roxy also hadn't made a reappearance, and that made me nervous, knowing she could reappear at a moment's notice.

Almost as if she'd heard me, Roxy materialized near Nia, throwing a magical blast at Aura that knocked them off course, sending them into disarray. Nia recovered quickly, a water whip blasting out from her as she fought. I started toward them, wanting to make sure no one else got hurt, when a cry of pain rang out over the noise, piercing straight through my heart. *Lily.*

My stomach dropped as I turned to look, my heart leaping into my throat as I saw Lexi, her red fur stained dark with blood. Lily's smaller form struggled beneath Lexi as she bared her teeth, trying her best to rip Lily's throat out. Without even thinking, I bolted toward them, lightning already springing to my palms as I went. I lashed out, power flowing from my hands, but I was too late, her teeth already sinking deep into Lily's neck as the blast connected with her, causing her to drop Lily in a heap on the floor.

In my weakened state the strike didn't do nearly what I wanted, and Lexi was quick to recover, her menacing gaze on me, Lily's blood staining her mouth. I looked at my prone friend, a slight tremor the only sign she was still alive. A deafening rage erupted in my soul with a hatred so intense I'd never felt before. With a primal growl, I lunged toward Lexi, my mind set on revenge and protecting Lily.

I was feet away from Lexi when lightning struck the ground in front of me, and I barely had enough time to react and dodge out of the way, rolling into a tumble on the ground before standing back up. I risked a glance to my left, Cas's smug face staring back at me from where he stood. I'd let myself get too distracted, and I froze.

"Keep going, Rowan!" Oliver yelled behind me, as he threw a burst of fire at Cas, who had no choice but to block, turning his attention to the halfling witch as he threw lightning back. Callan's sleek form darted past Oliver as he went after Cas.

A growl yanked my attention back to Lexi as she readied to go back for a strike to Lily's throat, who struggled to move, trying to pull herself up but falling back weakly on the ground with a whine. Lexi made eye contact with me, a wolfy grin splitting her face as she moved to strike.

"NO!" I shouted, sending a blast of lightning faster than I ever had before, pouring as much strength as I could into it, blasting Lexi away from Lily into a crumpled heap on the floor. She didn't move. I continued to run forward, muscles burning, as I stopped by Lily, leaning down to check on my friend. My heightened hearing picked up a heartbeat, weak but still there.

"Nia!" I shouted. An alarming amount of blood pooled under Lily, her eyelids fluttering weakly as she tried to lift her head up. "Stay down. Nia is going to heal you, and then you're going to be just fine. I promise." My voice cracked as I looked at her, all her usual sass and personality hidden under her injuries. I didn't know how severe her injuries would have to be for her healing not to save her, but judging by the amount of blood she'd lost, she was toeing that line. I couldn't lose another one. Not Lily. I turned my head desperately to look behind me, relief filling me as I saw Nia and Wolfe bounding toward us, Aura not far behind.

"Watch out!" Wolfe shouted as they continued running, and I whipped my head forward. Lexi's wolf stood on all fours, her eyes narrowed with pure hatred as she shook her head out, throwing off the remnants of my blast. She eyed Lily on the ground, before lolling her tongue out of her mouth, taunting me. *Look what I did*, her expression seemed to say.

I stood unsteadily, bringing my dagger forward as I stepped in front of Lily protectively. I called to my magic but managed nothing more than a few sparks in my spent state. Looks like I was going to have to do this the old-fashioned way. Her eyes zeroed in on my sparking fingertips and she ran toward me, wanting to take advantage of my weakness. Not wanting her to get near Lily, I followed her lead, running straight for her. Thoughts of Callan raced through my mind as we collided.

I leaned into my shifter powers as much as possible, spurring my reflexes but holding my human shape. Lexi slashed at me with tooth and claw as I did the same with my dagger, each of us leaving marks on the other. The wounds she'd left on my arm earlier protested in pain as new ones joined them, but I fought viciously, using my agility to my advantage as her larger figure struggled to twist and turn to keep up with me.

My knife sliced into her hind leg, and she cried out in pain but didn't back down, instead twisting her body to the side, barreling into me and knocking us both to the ground, the knife slipping from my grasp. She recovered faster, wasting no time in getting on top of me, her claws piercing through my shirt. My arms were pinned against her chest as I tried to push her off. I craned my neck away from her teeth as she tried to bite my face off, my muscles straining with the effort. I looked for help, but my friends were too far away to make it in time. I was on my own.

A loud roar cut across the clearing and my eyes darted to Callan, who was distracted in his own fight against Cas as he saw the predicament I was in. Cas took advantage of the opening, blasting Callan in his side as Oliver swooped in to deflect Cas.

Above me, Lexi growled, saliva dripping from her mouth onto my face as she pushed against me. I called to my lightning again, drawing on whatever it would give me, small sparks shooting out of my hands and attacking her face. It was enough of a disturbance that she let up a few inches, and I was able to dip my arm down, reaching for the dagger. My fingertips just barely brushed the cold steel as I tried to keep away from her teeth, unable to grip it.

'You smell like him,' her voice was in my head, and I struggled to focus on her words as I simultaneously tried to keep her at bay, my body quivering with the continued effort. It wasn't the first time she'd said that to me, her words when I was imprisoned echoing back to me.

"Go fuck yourself," I grunted out. Now was not the time for stupid conversation.

'*I don't mind,*' she giggled into my head, high-pitched and childlike. '*I always knew he would find his mate someday.*'

That got my attention, struggle be damned. "What did you just say?" The thread of fate that I could see between Lexi and Callan was still there, still the same tattered and broken connection it had been before, but still tethered.

My eyes flicked to Callan, who had recovered from his fight, trying to make his way toward me but Cas kept pulling him back in. Our eyes met, but it didn't matter. He wouldn't be able to save me. No one would get there in time, and my arms were getting weaker. I had to do whatever it took to get her off of me. Even if it could get him killed.

'*Don't worry. When I kill you, it'll be quick. Cas wants to keep you alive, but I think it's better with a little chaos. I won't rip your heart out torturously slow like I did that little bird girl, or we'd be here all night. She was a feisty one.*'

Blind feminine rage was a great motivator. Rage-fueled energy burst inside of me, and I dug deep within myself to try and find whatever I had left. There, a tiny sparking energy inside of me. I clung to it, demanded it come to me. The small amount obeyed, flowing to the surface as black dots danced across my vision, threatening to pull me under. Could I die from using too much magic?

I was about to find out.

My fingers sparked, and she yelped in pain as it connected with her face. She let up a few inches, and I took advantage of the distraction, dipping my arm further down until I felt the dagger hilt firmly in my hand. I wrapped my hand around it, barely able to wedge it between us as she renewed her intensity on trying to rip out my throat.

Unable to move my hands much further, I channeled energy instead, urging it to go through the dagger, no idea if it would actually work or not. Both of our eyes widened when it did, the electricity already sparking toward her. As the power got bigger, she shifted, and it was just enough space that I could pull my arm out, and I thrust the charged dagger into her rib cage with all my strength. She cried out but I didn't let go, staring into her eyes as I channeled as much lightning into her body as I could. My vision went red, blind in my anger, the scent of burnt flesh assaulting my nose.

I expected to pass out, my magic to cut off when the well was tapped, but instead my hand burned hotter, the metal of the dagger's hilt heating up until it was so hot I almost dropped it. Lexi's eyes widened as her body seized, and I watched in amazement as her fur started to fade, her limbs elongating into their human form as she slowly transformed back into human. She struggled against me, a strangled scream pulling from her mouth. The well of power inside me increased, swelling until I couldn't handle it anymore and it ripped into my arm, rushing through the knife and into Lexi. I tried to cut it off, tried to hold back, but I couldn't. Vibrations echoed in my hand as the dagger hilt burned hotter, before completely breaking apart into sharp pieces that sliced into my palm.

A deafening explosion ripped through the clearing, carrying the weight of an invisible force that no one stood a chance against, a benevolent firestorm. It was as if the very air had ignited, the sheer power of it sending everyone in the clearing hurtling backward. The air itself seemed to turn a fiery shade of crimson as it surged and billowed outward. Even more impressive, the cloud seemed to suck away all the magic.

From everyone except for me.

The elemental Fae powers failed, the witches' hands didn't glow, and the shifters seized, triggering their shifts back to human form.

As I watched, the bond connecting Lexi to Callan snapped, eating itself until it disintegrated into nothingness. A sharp pain erupted in my center, and I arched backward. My peripheral picked up a similar reaction in Callan as he finished his shift, and for a brief second, I wondered if we had been struck by a god.

The pain subsided, and I looked down, marveling as an intricate tether formed, weaving a mesmerizing pattern that stretched across the clearing, ending in Callan's chest. Our eyes met, mirror images of shock and confusion, and I knew he could see it too.

Lexi slumped against me, pulling my attention away from Callan, smoke rising from her bare body, and I knew she was dead. I shrugged her off to one side, taking careful notice not to rest my eyes on her scarred face. A weight was in my hand, and I looked down, my eyes going wide in shock.

My fingers closed around the intricate ring that sat in my palm, a few remnants of the dagger hilt littering its surface. The band was a deep midnight, so dark it resembled the night sky. Swirling patterns were engraved on the outside, that seemed to come alive as they circled the band, a glittering trail. Nestled at the heart of the ring was a multifaceted stone, just as inky as the band, but speckled with tiny pinpoints of light, like stars. It pulsed with an inner radiance, a beauty I struggled to take my eyes off of.

Staring at it, I couldn't resist the urge, and I slipped the ring onto my finger and instantly, I felt stronger. Powerful.

And I knew exactly what to do with it.

CHAPTER TWENTY-SEVEN

I stood, not sparing Lexi another glance. Nia had recovered quickly from the blast, already weaving her healing spell over Lily. Wolfe kneeled beside her, gently patting Lily's head and whispering soothing words to her. Beyond them, Oliver and Callan were back to engaging with Cas, who was sporting a new cut on his face, his clothes singed and dirty. They were in a standoff, all of them exhausted.

I strode closer. All three pairs of eyes dropped straight to my finger where the ring rested, a slow smile breaking across Cas's face. "Give it to me, Olette! Give me the ring, and this can all be over with."

I thrust my arms out, calling the wealth of power that resided in me to my command. It was easy. It flowed through to my palms, and I gasped at the color. My magic had always been yellow before, but now it was wrapped with a dark blue haze, a coolness settling over it as it crackled. Was this . . . Callan?

"True mates," Oliver whispered, I think more to himself than anything.

"Oh, that's just great." Cas barked a laugh, throwing out an overdramatic eye roll. "True mates with the rogue. Of course." I tried to wrap my head around what he was saying, my mind racing with millions of questions. How could Callan be my true mate when he had already been mated to Lexi? Was it possible for someone to have more than one mate?

"You're done, Cas. Your halfling is dead. You're stuck on this side of the realm." We circled in on him and he took a step back, keeping a close eye on my lightning hands that were primed to go at full force.

His eyes flickered to a spot behind my head, and I tensed, just as a loud explosion rocked the earth and we were all knocked off center. Cas took advantage of the distraction, calling a strike of lightning down and beaming himself up with it. We turned, Roxy standing behind us, throwing magical charms that exploded upon impact. Cas appeared right behind her. We fired shots at them, but another witch ran up to join their side, her dark hair billowing in the wind as she threw her hands up, casting a wide shimmering shield. We branched out, and I threw blast after blast at it with no success, but it was no use.

Roxy weaved her hands, a large portal opening in front of her. They wasted no time, the shield staying up as Cas and the witch jumped through. Roxy locked eyes with me, her dark eyes twinkling before she jumped through the portal. Seconds later it snapped shut, and the world fell quiet. Roxy had been a halfling this whole time. *Cunty bitch.*

With Cas gone, I slid the ring off of my finger, slipping it into my pocket for now. The second it left my skin, my exhaustion came flooding back into me, and I plopped my ass down right on the ground.

"I need to check on the others," Wolfe said as he stood from where Lily was still being healed, Nia still hard at work on her. He ran off to the rest of the pack, but the fight was pretty much over. With the addition of Aura and Varus, they'd made quick work of the rest of the enemies.

Sweat beaded down Nia's forehead as she worked. Lily's change had also been triggered by the spell from the ring, and I could see some of the life come back into her complexion as Nia worked. She would be okay.

I felt a presence behind me, and I craned my neck backward to look, regretting it almost immediately as I looked upward into Callan's nakedness from where he towered above me. "Happy to see me?" I quipped as I rotated away. He was a beautiful man, but no man looked good from that angle.

A surge of emotion rushed through me. Confusion, lust, anger, and the strongest one, happiness. Something suspiciously akin to love. But none of these emotions were mine. I felt them, but like they were outside of my heart, just on the outskirts.

"I can feel you," Callan whispered, pulling me up to my full height as he scanned my face. His eyes glazed over, and suddenly he wasn't looking at me. He was looking *through* me as he rooted through the same emotions I was feeling. These weren't mine.

They were *his*.

"I don't understand," he whispered as he touched a hand to my cheek cautiously.

"Does this mean you're not going to die?" I asked stupidly. I was so tired; it was hard to even form coherent sentences.

He laughed, the freest sound I had ever heard him make, both hands coming up to cup my face as he leaned down, planting a soft kiss on my forehead. "I don't know what it means, but I think I like it."

WE SAT OUTSIDE THE INFIRMARY WHILE WE WAITED FOR Lily to wake up, discussing what had happened. Bloodied and bruised, we took turns getting healing magic from Nia as she did her best to help everyone out without exerting too much of her energy. She'd done as much as she could for Lily, and now she just needed to sleep it off.

"What does this mean? How can we be mates?" I directed my

question to Finn, but it was Oliver who spoke. I sat next to Callan on the couch, his hand placed protectively on my lower back. He'd barely let me out of his sight since the fight ended, but I wasn't complaining. I hadn't been able to feel his emotions since the field, and I wondered if it only reacted to strong emotions. Or maybe he had learned to block me out?

"You can feel each other, yes?" Oliver gave us a hard stare, looking from one to the other.

I nodded.

"Have you had any shared dreams?"

I shook my head, but Callan nodded yes. "What, when?" I asked incredulously.

"It wasn't a dream, but you came to me that one night. Right before I joined you in the Faerie realm. I'd call it more of an apparition."

My eyes widened as the memory of the dream came floating back to me. "That was real?"

"Definitely true mates," Oliver said matter-of-factly, leaning back in his chair to rest his tired bones. "True mates share a connection over everything else, a bond determined by the soul, between a Fae and their partner. There haven't been many, not much is known about them really, except that the connection is stronger than anyone can ever experience otherwise. Connected in life, and in death."

"But how could that be? He had a mate. Lexi was his mate; I saw their bond."

"It's impossible for one to have more than one mate. There is no room in the soul."

"Then how?" I pressed. What if this bond with Callan was some sort of residual effect of the ring, which still burned a hole in my pocket. We all sat there, no one having a suggestion. I wracked my brain over our fight, and Lexi's words came floating back to me, words I didn't understand in the heat of the moment. I leaned forward, everyone's eyes on me.

"When I was fighting her, she said something to me. Right

before I . . . killed her." I hesitated on the words, the realization of what I'd done sinking in. Whether or not she deserved it, I'd still taken someone's life. "She said, 'I always knew he'd find his mate.'"

Callan frowned, his head cocking to the side. I knew he was reading me, reading my emotions, and the more I thought about that, the more I didn't like it. I needed to learn how to create a wall between these bonds. No one should ever have to know exactly how someone else is feeling.

"That implies she didn't think she was his," Finn said, his brow knitted.

"I recognized one of those witches," Wolfe interjected, his face pinched in anger. After the battle had ended, we'd tallied losses. We'd killed all the enemy except the ones who escaped, but we'd lost ten of our own. We'd won the battle, but it sure didn't feel like it, especially for the Alpha of the pack. "The dark-haired one. I've seen her before."

"Where?" Callan commanded.

Wolfe ran a hand through his hair, letting out a calming breath. "In Montana. She worked closely with the Supreme in a lot of situations." The Supreme Alpha, otherwise known as Wolfe's dad. One of Cas's witches did business with the leader of all the North American shifters. I knew witches worked for the highest bidder, but was it too much of a coincidence?

"Callan," I said, turning to him. A theory was forming in my mind, something that I wouldn't be able to shake if I didn't ask. "What pack did Lexi come from when you were mated? Was she in the Clover pack?"

"No, the Clover pack was already my pack," he said, sharing a serious look with Wolfe, who would have been his beta at the time. "Our mate bond was discovered at the annual shifter summit in Montana. She was in the Supreme's pack, and I brought her back with me."

"Motherfucker!" Wolfe exploded, standing up and punching

the wall behind him in his anger. "I knew he was a piece of shit, but this? That's taking it too far!"

"What would he have to gain from spelling me a fake mate bond?" Callan asked, the cogs in his mind churning as he thought.

"You were strong, Callan. He was one of the strongest Alphas in centuries, and you did not like conforming to his rules. Don't you remember? You butted heads constantly."

"So maybe he was afraid of your power?" Nia offered, her strategic mind already working out the details of what would make the most sense. "She killed your whole pack, didn't she? The catalyst of you being outcast?" I raised my eyebrow at her, and she smiled sheepishly. "Lily likes to gossip."

"If he went in league with dark witches just to knock Callan out, then he's an idiot. Messing with mate bonds is seriously dark magic, forbidden among our kind. To do that is . . . disgusting. Unforgivable," Oliver said.

"So what do we do?"

"I need to go there and talk to him. Get to the bottom of this." Wolfe was pacing back and forth now, his hulking figure already taking up much of the sparse free space there was in the small waiting room.

"We also have my psycho Fae family trying to hunt me down for the ring." Something occurred to me, and I frowned. "How did I get the ring anyway? It was in the dagger you gave me, Callan. Did you know it was there this whole time?"

It seemed the only likely explanation. He'd made the dagger out of the gearshift of my old car, so he had to have known something was inside of it. "No, I had no idea." I used one end of my bond, and this time his emotions did surge through. Confusion, but no deceit.

"What urged you to make the knife?" Oliver asked intently.

"I . . . dreamt about it. After that day you told me how much the car meant to you." I blushed, looking away like a giddy schoolgirl and hating myself for it. His hand stayed hot against my back. "I dreamt exactly how to make it, and when I woke up, I did."

Oliver scratched his bearded chin. "It's most likely spelled to you then, Rowan. I'm not sure how you managed that, but the ring is powerful, stronger than all of us combined. If the ring wanted to be near you, it would find a way. That would explain why Olette didn't feel the need to remember where it was."

"Who could have put such a spell on it?"

"I don't know. To spell something of this magnitude, you'd need an incredibly powerful magic user."

"Cas will need time to recover. Now that you know how to wield the ring, you are significantly more powerful than he is. They need to think very carefully about their next move, as we have the upper hand." This came from Finn, who had been fairly quiet since the fight. I often felt his eyes on me, but when I met them, I couldn't fathom his expression, his light eyes shuttered.

"I don't think any of us should stay in the pack for now," Wolfe said seriously, the sorrow of his losses etching a pattern in his face. "I've arranged for the remaining members to stay with the other nearby packs, at least until this is all over so we can stay here until we recover. If Cas comes back, we won't have to worry about them getting hurt."

"I'm so sorry," I told him, my eyes pleading with him for forgiveness even though my heart told me I didn't deserve it. "If it wasn't for me, this never would have happened."

"Never be sorry, Rowan." He gave me a kind smile that didn't quite reach his eyes. "I'd repeat every choice we made. We fight for our own, and you are one of ours for as long as you want to be."

"Now that we have them regrouping," Nia said, her voice soft yet commanding, "we should go on the offensive. We have the ring. We have Rowan. Let's kill Queen Tantaii."

"It won't be that easy," Finn countered, playing devil's advocate. "Now that Rowan has the means, the Queen isn't going to be easy to access. She has Cas, who we failed to kill might I add, and Primoris is not an easy stronghold to penetrate. We got there easy enough through the tunnels, but that was just the outskirts. We'd never be able to tunnel our way close enough to reach the castle. No, we'd need to draw her out somehow."

"If we can trick her into thinking she can get the ring, she'll come out," I said, and I knew that was true. I couldn't remember any interactions with the Queen besides the one, but I knew she was power-hungry, and hopefully overconfident. If she thought she had me beat, she would show. But we needed to be sure we could kill her when she did. We weren't ready.

"We need to figure this out first," Wolfe said. "That witch is connected to the Supreme Alpha. And if the Supreme Alpha is in line with Cas's forces, then we need to nip that shit in the bud. It will be much harder to beat them if they can turn our own forces against us too, if we're corrupt from the top down. We're going to Montana."

Chapter Twenty-Eight

When Lily's beautiful brown eyes opened again, I was the only one in the room. I'd kicked everyone out, including a livid Nia, and sent them all to get some sleep. She'd been swaying on her feet with all the people she was healing. Any longer and we might have had eleven casualties.

"Rowan?" she asked weakly as she gingerly sat herself up in the bed.

A grin split my face as I looked at my friend, just grateful she was even alive. "Hey there."

"I feel like I've been hit by a truck," she groaned. "What happened?"

"Lexi happened, that's what. She almost killed you."

"That raging bitch! When I get my hands on her—"

"She's dead," I said, cutting her off. I was grateful my voice didn't shake. Truly, I hated Lexi, but the rush of power had been intoxicating, and I hated that it felt like that. Taking a life should never feel good, but it had. "I killed her."

Lily's eyes were wide as saucers as she looked me over. It'd been hours since the battle had ended, but still I wore my blood-stained clothes, not ready to head back toward my cabin. When I'd kicked everyone out, Callan had left begrudgingly, and I had no doubt he'd gone back to my cabin instead of his. I wasn't quite ready to be alone with him yet.

I'd barely become accustomed to the whole idea of having mates, and now I found out I had a true mate, who was connected to my soul. I should be happy, and I was, but I was also nervous. What if all the feelings I'd been having for Callan had only been because of the bond? And what did this mean for us? I wasn't ready to jump in, settle down and get married and pop out little panther babies. We hadn't even said we loved each other yet.

"That's badass."

"No, Nia is badass. You'd be six feet under right now if we didn't have her."

"She is, isn't she?" The wistfully dreamy expression on her face almost made me gag, but I was happy for her. What was happening between them was natural, it was easy. It wasn't back and forth, fire and ice. She cleared her throat, and I reached over, handing her the cup of water that was a bit out of her reach. "Is Callan okay? They were mates."

A blush creeped up my neck as my words froze.

"Rowan?"

"Their mate bond broke when she died, and it seems we are true mates." I looked anywhere but at her. "A new bond formed, and I can feel what he feels and vice versa. I think I hate it."

"WHAT!" she shrieked loudly, making me jump. "Ohmygodohmygodohmygod!"

"Relax," I told her, my voice hushed. "And also, we had sex."

Lily's mouth gaped open like a fish. "Like, just now?"

"No," I rolled my eyes. "Before we got attacked. I was trying to sneak away."

"I figured you might try to do something like that," she said with a disapproving glare. "Well, I'm glad you changed your mind. We needed you. And I'm *so* happy for you and Callan. When's the mating ceremony?"

Lily passed out again after about an hour, exhausted from her ordeal. Waiting until she fell asleep, I slipped out into the now darkness, tracing the shadows that lined the different buildings with my feet, in no hurry to get back to my cabin.

I was halfway there when I saw a large figure in a grassy opening to my side. Familiar red eyes glowed brightly as they watched me, and I trotted over, eager to delay my one one-on-one with Callan.

"You came back."

'Indeed, I did,' Varus spoke into my mind. *'Lithia is dead. The shadow beasts went for her first, while we were all sleeping. She couldn't heal fast enough.'*

My heart clenched tightly as the sorrow washed over me. Another one dead.

"I'm so sorry," I told him. "I don't blame you for leaving, by the way."

'Aura gave me an earful. She might have killed me herself if I didn't come help.' His tone was bitter. *'Not that I have much to live for anymore.'*

"I'm grateful you did. You saved many lives." I tried to steer him back toward the positive. I'd seen firsthand how horrible losing your mate could be with Elowen and Kai. I hoped the same thing didn't happen to Varus. He was surly, and a bully, but I liked him.

'You better get home, little one. The panther grows restless.'

I sighed, knowing he was right. It was time to face my fears.

THE DOOR TO THE CABIN CREAKED AS I STEPPED INTO the dimly lit room. My heart leaped in my throat as I took in the room.

"Candles?" I choked out. "Where did you even find candles? I don't have candles in my cabin."

Romantic lighting emanated from the entire living room, an elegant candle perched on every available surface. The soft glow of their light illuminated Callan's face with shadows from where he sat on my couch.

"I called in a favor."

"It's beautiful," I told him. "But I do think we need to talk."

"You already talk too much," he said, but I felt the knife of anxiety that shot through our bond that we shared.

"That," I said, giving a pointed look in the direction of his chest, "is a big part of the reason why. I know mates are what you know, but this is new to me. I want to do this, don't get me wrong. But I need to go at my own pace. And I need my own independence."

A look of hurt crossed his face. "Do you think I wouldn't allow you to be your own person?"

"I don't like anyone having any control of me, and you being able to feel my emotions is exactly that."

"Then we learn how to block it." He ran a hand through his dark hair. "I know we butt heads a lot, but I'm not here to dictate your boundaries. I'll follow your lead."

I sighed, relaxing into the couch, thankful he was letting me keep the control. We stayed silent for a moment before his fingertips started tracing a lazy trail on my arm, just the right amount of pressure to give me goosebumps. He leaned forward, bringing his lips to my ear.

"Before we learn to block it out, can we try something?" His voice was low, thick with need, and I couldn't say no. Arousal burned brightly through our bond as I descended my lips to his in a passionate kiss. I kicked a leg over him, straddling him on the couch, never missing a beat with my tongue. Hands tugged at my shirt, and within seconds it was ripped in half, falling onto the floor with a soft thump.

"Hey!" I complained against his mouth.

"It was ruined anyway," he mumbled. "We're disgusting."

"You're right, let me take a shower," I said, pulling back and motioning to get off him, but firm hands pulled me back in place and I gasped as I was yanked back against him.

"Allow me," he said, and with a firm flex of his muscles we were standing, my arms gripped around his neck so I had something to hang on to. His lips found mine again, and I moaned against his tongue, my hips rocking forward of their own accord. Before I knew it, we were stepping into the shower, my back thudding solidly against the cold tile wall, and I shrieked.

The spray of the shower sounded, and I expected to get pelted with cold water, but only Callan was in my vision, his eyes blazing a path straight to my heart as he blocked the spray from touching me. I wiggled and he let me down as steam began to rise in the shower. I made quick work of the rest of my clothes, throwing them out and onto the bathroom floor as Callan did the same.

In seconds, we were back in each other's arms, his hard length pressing against me as he let the water cascade over us both, washing away the marks of the day's battle. His hand slid between us, exploring, before coming up to furiously circle my clit.

"You're so wet for me," he teased, and I whimpered with need. Our bond was brighter than ever, his emotions flooding through me, heightening my arousal. Each touch of his skin on mine left a blazing trail of heat.

"Fuck me," I begged, needing him now. "I can't wait." He chuckled into my mouth, gripping my hips, and spinning me around to face the wall. My forearms came forward to brace myself as he surged into me, one hand coming around to resume its work on my clit. I screamed, a small orgasm ripping through me as soon as he entered, the flash of the bond too much pleasure to withstand.

"Oh my god," I groaned, my head falling forward to lean

against the shower wall as he continued to thrust into me. I moved my hips back to match his thrusts, another wave retreating into a tsunami. My legs shook and he withdrew, flipping me back to face him so quickly that I almost slipped. He dropped my arms around his neck, then bent down and lifted me up around his waist, sliding back into me with one quick move as he backed me against the tile. His head came down to my neck, nipping and suckling as I panted in time with his thrusts.

He reared back, slowing his pace down slightly as he pulled all the way out, looking down at our bodies before slamming all the way back in. "You take me so well," he groaned softly before he captured my mouth once again, my nails scratching marks into his back. My teeth sank into his shoulder as I came again, squeezing my walls tightly around his cock. Callan shouted and our bond blazed brightly, my body flooding with emotion so intense it split me apart, sending me further over the edge than I'd ever thought possible. He came with me, burying his head in my shoulder as he let out the sexiest moan I had ever heard.

Slowly he released me, allowing me to slide down his body gently and stand on shaky legs under the warm spray of the shower. "That was—"

"Incredible," I finished for him, barely starting to catch my breath. "Is that what you wanted to try?"

He picked up my cheetah print loofah that was hanging from the temperature nozzle, squirting some vanilla-scented body wash before lathering it up. He motioned for me, and I shivered as he started gently washing my body, removing the last remnants of the challenging day we'd had. His touch was soothing, and he gently kneaded my tired muscles and tender skin from my newly healed wounds. I'd barely felt them with everything that had been going on. He leaned down, kissing a spot at the nape of my neck.

"I have a few more things we could try out too."

Afterword

Thank you for sticking with me for the next installment of Rowan's journey!

As I sit here writing this way too past my bedtime, I am left feeling nothing but gratitude. Gratitude that I get to wake up in the morning is always the first one, but the second is gratitude that there are people like you out there, wanting to read this book. I can't help but feel like the luckiest author in the world.

This one was almost an easier book to write. Rowan gets louder and louder in my head every day, and she won't rest until her story is finished. I loved diving into the Faerie realm and getting to know their way of life. Fantasy will always be my first love, and I hope to bring you even more of stories like that.

Thank you for reading. Thank you for liking, sharing, recommending, discussing, and even thinking about the books that I write. Thank you for existing. I hope you enjoyed this one. Can't wait to be back for more.

Love always,

Sav

About the Author

Savannah is a California native and Las Vegas dweller. She was that kid that went to class with a stack full of books and paid absolutely no attention to the teacher. After reading her way through the library and not seeing the stories she wanted, she decided to write her own!

Savannah Lee writes 18+ mature urban fantasy and paranormal romance stories.

Join my Facebook group!
Savannah Lee's Silly Rabbits

Instagram
@savannahleeauthor

TikTok
@savannahleewrites

Goodreads
https://www.goodreads.com/author/show/6540743.
Savannah_Lee

Follow me on Amazon!
https://www.amazon.com/stores/Savannah-Lee/author/
B0C4KK3954

ALSO BY SAVANNAH LEE

CLOVER PACK SERIES

Midnight Mated #1

Midnight Magic #2

Midnight Mayhem #3

Made in the USA
Monee, IL
22 December 2023

48252062R00142